'What c... a?'

She exhaled shakily at the sound of Roman's voice and had to bring herself back to a reality that had expanded beyond her wildest imaginings.

'I hardly know what I want,' she admitted honestly. 'I don't even know what I can have.'

'Try to tell me,' Roman coaxed. 'Search your deepest fantasies and tell me what you'd like me to do.'

They were standing by the bed. Roman was holding her with his chin resting lightly on her head.

'You have to spell it out, Eva.'

'You like to hear it?' she guessed.

'Maybe,' he admitted.

'Touch me,' she whispered.

'I am touching you, Eva.'

Yes, and her bones were melting. But it wasn't enough. Roman knew that—just as she knew there was more…if she could only bring herself to ask. But for once in her headstrong, outspoken life she couldn't find the words.

Susan Stephens was a professional singer before meeting her husband on the tiny Mediterranean island of Malta. In true Mills & Boon® Modern™ Romance style they met on Monday, became engaged on Friday, and were married three months after that. Almost thirty years and three children later, they are still in love. (Susan does not advise her children to return home one day with a similar story, as she may not take the news with the same fortitude as her own mother!)

Susan had written several non-fiction books when fate took a hand. At a charity costume ball there was an after-dinner auction. One of the lots, 'Spend a Day with an Author', had been donated by Mills & Boon® author Penny Jordan. Susan's husband bought this lot, and Penny was to become not just a great friend but a wonderful mentor, who encouraged Susan to write romance.

Susan loves her family, her pets, her friends and her writing. She enjoys entertaining, travel, and going to the theatre. She reads, cooks, and plays the piano to relax, and can occasionally be found throwing herself off mountains on a pair of skis or galloping through the countryside.

Visit Susan's website at www.susanstephens.net—she loves to hear from her readers all around the world!

Recent titles by the same author:

DIAMOND IN THE DESERT*
TAMING THE LAST ACOSTA**
THE MAN FROM HER WAYWARD PAST**
A TASTE OF THE UNTAMED**

*linked to the Skavanga family. Visit their website at:
http://www.susanstephens.com/skavanga/index.html
***all linked to the Acosta family.*

THE FLAW IN HIS DIAMOND

BY
SUSAN STEPHENS

Published in Great Britain 2014
by Mills & Boon, an imprint of Harlequin (UK) Limited,
Eton House, 18-24 Paradise Road, Richmond, Surrey, TW9 1SR

ISBN: 978 0 263 90814 5

Harlequin (UK) Limited's policy is to use papers that are natural, renewable and recyclable products and made from wood grown in sustainable forests. The logging and manufacturing processes conform to the legal environmental regulations of the country of origin.

Printed and bound in Spain
by Blackprint CPI, Barcelona

THE FLAW IN HIS DIAMOND

To everyone in the wonderful team
at Harlequin Mills and Boon
who make writing so much fun

CHAPTER ONE

'SO. WHAT DO we know about him?' Leaning her hands, palms flat, on her no-nonsense scrubbed pine table, Eva glared, first at her older, married sister, Britt, and then at her younger sister, Leila.

Leila's cheeks flushed pink, though she was used to Eva ranting. Leila's middle sister was strong. And that was a polite way of putting it. Eva was also one hell of a pain in the neck when she was in one of her campaigning moods as she was now. Leila adored both her sisters, though she sometimes wished Eva could find a man and move out of the family home, taking her emotional pyrotechnics with her. How tranquil would life be then? Leila could only dream. But would anyone take Eva on? Both Leila and Britt had tried to interest the available men in Skavanga in Eva by extolling the many virtues of their firebrand sister, but none of the men had been interested in taking Eva anywhere, unless it was for a game of pool or darts. They had countered Leila and Britt's glowing recommendations by reminding them about Eva's famous temper and how loud she could shout, before turning their attention to quieter, more amenable companions.

'Come on!' Eva rapped, standing straight and planting her hands on her hips. 'I need answers here. It's all right for you, Britt—married to the Black Sheikh, one of the leading lights in the consortium. I don't expect you to compromise your loyalties by having an opinion. But you, Leila? Shame. On. You. I'm surprised you can't see that, if we allow them to, the consortium will happily rampage over our polar landscape and then move on. And don't tell me I'm overreacting. That's what will happen if one of us doesn't make a stand.'

That was the thing about Eva, Leila mused as she removed herself to a quiet place in her head. Eva could have an argument all by herself without anyone else even taking part.

'I won't let the consortium have everything its own way, even if you will,' Eva continued heatedly, 'and before you say a word, Britt, let me make this quite clear. I might have seen our family business stolen from under our noses by three unscrupulous men but, unlike you, I have no intention of sleeping with one of them to make me feel better—'

'That's enough,' Leila cut in with unusual fire. 'Have you forgotten your sister is married to Sheikh Sharif?'

Shaking her head, Leila smiled an apology on behalf of Eva to Britt, who shrugged. Both sisters were accustomed to Eva's tirades. What Eva needed was a curb on that temper. Her heart was in the right place, but their sister rarely thought before she spoke—or acted. And that was far more worrying, as far as Leila was concerned.

'Well, you two are utterly useless,' Eva exploded as her sisters continued sipping their coffee and reading their newspapers, and generally concentrating on other things as they waited for Eva's tirade to burn itself out.

Tossing back her flame-red explosion of waist-length curls, Eva picked up the newspaper, her frown deepening as she scanned the latest developments at the mine, spearheaded by the man she had had her knife into since her nemesis, Roman Quisvada, had first shocked her into silence at Britt's wedding with his swarthy good looks and inflexible manner.

'*Count* Roman Quisvada?' she intoned scathingly. 'Well, that's a ridiculous name to begin with.'

'He's Italian, Eva,' Britt murmured patiently as she carried on reading her newspaper. 'And he's a bona fide count. It's an ancient title—'

'Count? My foot!' Eva scoffed. 'He can count how many pickets I'm going to assemble at the mine. That should keep him busy *counting*!'

'And I believe he's quite strong-minded,' Britt observed mildly, flashing a glance at Leila.

'He's the same guy I slammed the door on at your wedding?' Eva peered at Roman's image in the press. 'As I remember it, he didn't take much scaring off on that occasion.'

'You can stop rubbing your hands with glee at the thought of taking him on again,' Leila warned. 'When you met him at the wedding, it was the door to the bridal suite you shut in his face, so you could hardly expect him to stick his foot in and demand entry.'

'Anyone would think he'd made an impression on you, Eva,' Britt remarked as she laid down her newspaper. 'We're certainly wasting a lot of time and energy on him if he didn't.'

Eva gave a scornful huff. 'I just can't bear being pushed around, that's all.'

'We need the money, Eva,' Britt calmly pointed out.

'We must keep the consortium on board. We cannot afford to upset this man. The mine would have gone down without the consortium's investment, throwing hundreds of people out of work. Is that what you want?'

'Of course not,' Eva protested. 'But there has to be another way—a slower way, a careful way. Do you have any idea how many times I've asked this wretched man to meet with me so we can discuss my concerns about the speed of his drilling programme?'

'Discuss? Or lay down the law?' Britt demanded, cocking her chin to give her sister a look. Neither Britt nor Leila was frightened of Eva's outbursts, though, like Leila, Britt did dream of the day when Eva found a man who could provide an alternative channel for her passionate nature.

'He has to hear the truth from someone,' Eva stormed. 'And I speak Italian. So he'd got no excuse not to meet with me.'

'I believe the count speaks six languages,' Britt murmured mildly, which resulted in a contemptuous huff from Eva.

'Well, if you two won't take a stand, I will.'

'I knew we could rely on you,' Britt murmured wryly.

'Fresh coffee, anyone?' Leila, who always played the peacemaker, offered. She skirted round her middle sister as if Eva were a stick of dynamite waiting to blow.

But Eva wasn't finished yet. 'Just look at this,' she said, spreading out the local newspaper on the table. The centrefold featured a large photograph of Count Roman Quisvada, while the banner headline shrieked: COUNT RESCUES SKAVANGA in extra bold type. 'It makes it sound as if he saved us from disaster single-handed.'

'That's pretty much what he did do,' Britt observed,

lifting her chin to shoot a stare that curbed her sister's flow. 'Quisvada, Sharif and the third man, Raffa Leon, *have* saved Skavanga. And if you can't see that—'

'You don't even get a mention, Britt,' Eva pointed out. 'And you're supposed to be running the mine.'

'I *am* running the mine,' Britt confirmed. 'And the only reason they're making a fuss of the count is because they interviewed him when he visited the mine to see for himself how his orders were being carried out—'

'When he was too busy to see me, do you mean?' Eva demanded.

'He was obviously very busy seeing me,' Britt confirmed with a shrug and a wry glance at Leila.

'I'm sure the count was far too busy for distractions on that occasion,' Leila added gently.

'Oh, well, thanks a lot.' Eva chewed her lip as she stared at the photograph of her nemesis in the newspaper. 'Nice to know I qualify as a distraction. From what I can see in this article, the Skavanga family has been written out of the story altogether. All this female journalist wants to write about is Mr High and Mighty, Count Roman Quisvada.'

'Maybe because she was interviewing him?' Leila ventured.

'Maybe because she was in bed with him,' Eva countered sharply. 'I really don't care. To a man like that any woman is just another notch on his bedpost.'

'You wish,' Britt murmured.

'What was that?' Eva snapped, rounding on her older sister.

Shaking her head, Britt pressed her lips down, adopting an innocent expression as she exchanged a look with Leila, who was careful to show no emotion at all, in case it fuelled Eva's fire.

'He's a dangerous-looking individual, if you ask me,' Eva remarked, pushing the newspaper aside.

'Fortunately, we didn't ask you,' Britt said mildly.

'All hair grease and designer clothes, with a good helping of arrogance and entitlement,' Eva muttered, sliding a disparaging look at the count's photograph.

'Definitely no hair grease,' Britt argued. 'I would have noticed that. And secondly, if Sharif trusts the count with his life, then so do I.'

Eva narrowed her eyes as she contemplated, the conflict ahead of her. 'Well, I, for one, can't wait to meet up with him again.'

'I'm sure he feels exactly the same way about you,' Britt commented, tongue in cheek.

'I'm sure Eva will see sense, and reason with him,' Leila put in, clearly eager to calm things down.

'Reason?' Britt pulled a wry face. 'That's an interesting way of putting it. But just before you apply your version of reason to your exchanges with Roman, Eva, may I remind you that without his money and the money from the other two men in the consortium both our mine and the town would have died by now?'

'I haven't forgotten anything,' Eva assured her older sister. 'I just can't understand why he hasn't stayed here to see things through. Oh, I forgot,' she added acidly. 'He prefers to swan around on his private island.'

'He's on the island for the wedding of his cousin,' Britt pointed out.

'He could still have seen me before he went when I asked him to,' Eva insisted. 'If he had explained things clearly, perhaps we could all understand what's happening at the mine.'

'Perhaps if you had listened instead of protesting,' Britt suggested, but gently this time, because no one doubted Eva's genuine concern for the pristine landscape the new drilling was putting under threat. 'You can't expect him to drop everything to attend a meeting with you. He has a life, as well as all his other business interests. There are huge sums of money involved—'

'Oh, yes, it always boils down to money,' Eva observed with a dismayed shake of her head.

'I'm afraid it does,' Britt agreed calmly. 'We like to keep people in jobs around here.'

'That's all I care about,' Eva assured her sister. 'But I also care deeply about a land that has remained unchanged for millennia.'

'Why don't you talk to Roman face to face instead of discussing it with us?' Leila suggested.

'I've tried that.' Eva pulled a face. 'He won't see me.'

'For all the aforementioned reasons,' Britt said. 'But there's nothing to stop you trying again,' she pointed out, exchanging a hopeful look with Leila once she was sure Eva wasn't looking. They had both noticed the chemistry between Roman and Eva at the wedding as they fired angry glances at each other from opposite sides of the aisle. 'You never know, you might even get on better with him when you meet him again.'

'That's hardly likely,' Eva scoffed, tugging angry fingers through her tangle of red-gold hair. 'He's about as ready to listen to a woman like me as he is to eat tacks for breakfast.'

'You'll never know unless you try,' Leila pointed out as Britt got up to give Eva a reassuring hug.

'Come on,' Britt cajoled as she drew Eva into her arms. 'Don't get so upset about everything. Even you can't save the world single-handed.'

'But I can try.'

'That's right, you can—at least, your tiny bit of it,' Britt agreed.

'Then that's what I'm going to do,' Eva mumbled, her face buried in the shoulder of her older sister.

'What are you going to do?' Britt said suspiciously, holding Eva at arm's length so she could stare into her sister's eyes. 'Should we discuss this first?'

'No. I don't think we should,' Eva said, sniffing loudly as she took a pace back. 'No more coffee for me, thank you, Leila. I've got a trip to make.'

He never drank. He chose not to lose control. Ever. He had seized the opportunity during the champagne reception following the wedding ceremony to slip away. Everyone would be getting ready for the party in the evening, which gave him a chance to shower and change, and maybe take a refreshing dip in his pool.

He stopped where he always stopped on the cliff path. It was a place of particular significance to him, for it was here on his fourteenth birthday he had contemplated throwing the gold chain he wore around his neck into the sea. And then maybe he would follow, his youthful infuriated self had seethed impotently.

Thankfully, he had proved stronger than that, and had resisted the teenage impulse to vent his grief in a way that would hurt others as much as himself.

It was a hot day for a wedding. Shrugging off his formal jacket, he opened the neck of his shirt. His hand stole to the slim gold chain. His adoptive mother had given him the necklace on his birthday. That was the same day she explained to him haltingly that his real mother had died, and had wanted Roman to have her only decent piece of jewellery.

That was the first time he heard he had a 'real' mother. What else was the woman sitting in front of him? He could still remember his shock and the pain. Discovering his father was not his father, any more than the woman he adored was his mother, had been life-changing. His adoptive father had been furious to discover Roman had learned the truth about his birth, but the damage was done by then. His adoptive father had believed Roman would crumble now he knew the facts. His adoptive mother had argued with this, knowing how strong he was. He was her son just as much as he was the son of his blood mother, and she knew him.

He had stood here on the cliff, fierce as a lion on that day, full of the passions of youth, and then he had stormed home and demanded they tell him the truth—all of it. And so he had learned about his blood father, the count, the drunken gambler who had sold his son to the childless wife of a mafia don in settlement of his gambling debts.

'You're not blood so you can't take over the family business,' his adoptive father had thought it timely to explain while Roman was still reeling from these facts. 'But I couldn't love you more if you were my blood and so you will inherit my island and all my property, while your cousin takes over the business after me. Your job is to protect him—'

It was only then Roman had realised how fast he could turn off his emotions. He couldn't have cared less about owning an island, or inheriting a vast property portfolio. All he cared about was his life up to now having been a lie. He'd changed on that day. His adoptive mother accused him of becoming distant and aloof. Unreachable, his adoptive father had raged with frustration, hating to see his wife devastated by Roman's treatment of her.

Roman still carried the guilt to this day and wondered if his behaviour had hastened her death. He would never know, but sometimes he could still hear her gentle voice in his head, insisting that his blood mother had no choice, and that in those days, in their society, women had no choice but to do what the men told them.

Now he thought of those two women, his mother and his adoptive mother, as sisters beneath the skin, looking down on him. His only desire was to make them happy and proud of him.

An alarm on his phone jolted him back to the present. Scanning the screen, he pressed a key. Watching for a moment, he felt a surge of anger. It would take him half an hour to reach the palazzo from here if he stuck to the path, but not if he took a short cut.

CHAPTER TWO

SHE HAD NEARLY reached her destination and paused for a moment to catch her breath. She could see the count's magnificent home on the top of the cliff, a citadel of power glittering white and menacing in the heat haze. The steep path she was climbing snaked up a white cliff overlooking an azure sea. It might be someone's idea of a heavenly walk, but she was hot and sweaty and had to keep her mind firmly fixed on her goal and her reasons for coming here so that anger powered her steps.

Having researched the fastest route from Arctic Skavanga to the count's island, she had unfortunately given rather less thought to local topography, let alone the climate. And a hill was a hill was a hill, anywhere but here, it seemed, where the path to the count's eyrie was treacherous and packed with slippery shale.

Throwing herself down on a prickly bank, she threw her arm over her face. The sun was like a flaming torch and she hadn't even thought to bring a bottle of water with her from the plane. There had been very little forward planning. She had rushed into the trip after a furious row with Britt, during which she told her caring older sister to butt out and mind her own business—something she now felt sick and wretched about. Why did she always shoot off her mouth and then spend the rest of her time regretting it?

She had left without apologising, jumping on the first flight out of Skavanga. She caught a connecting flight to the Italian mainland, and from there a ferry to the count's private island. It was a ferry packed with exuberant wedding guests, all of whom were in a very different mood from her, though they'd got round her in the end. They were all so happy as they headed for what they described as the wedding of the year. She had ended up playing a round of darts with a group of older men, and had scored the winning double. She was one of the boys, they had assured her, patting her on the back as she glowed with pride.

Now she just glowed. All over.

Getting up, she brushed herself down and started determinedly up the cliff again. The closer she got to the palazzo, the faster her heart was beating. She wasn't frightened of anything or anyone, but just to herself she would admit she was a little bit scared of the count—mainly because she had never met anyone like him before. He'd towered over her at Britt's wedding, his face tough and battle-hardened. He was older than she was, and Roman centurion rather than Roman effete. She remembered the lips of a sensualist. She'd thought of little else since. His hair was glorious—too long, too thick, too black. Perfect. And his eyes were keen, dark and dangerous. He had a ridiculous amount of stubble on his swarthy cheeks, considering it couldn't have been long since he shaved when she met him. But it was that something behind his watchful eyes that had intrigued her, because that had hinted at something hidden and dangerous in his past.

She had to stop this. Was she trying to psyche herself out before she had even confronted him? Think fail and you would fail. That was Eva's motto. Think success, and at least you stood a chance.

He was strong. She was too. She did stand a chance of convincing him to slow down the drilling programme. Quisvada was also obscenely rich, and, though she disapproved of ostentatious displays of wealth, she couldn't deny a certain curiosity in seeing how the other half lived. All in all, safe had never been an option for her. She needed a challenge like this. She needed to leave the Arctic Circle and test herself in the wider world, and she cared so passionately about the mine this was her chance to prove it. There was no doubt in her mind. She would make Quisvada listen.

Shifting her backpack into a more comfortable position, she continued on up the path, wondering about the fluttering in her chest. What did she have to worry about? She was in no danger from the count. He was hardly her type—

No man is your type.

Having run out of things to argue with herself for the moment, she stopped again. It didn't help that she was overdressed. Her hectic decision to come here had ruled out sensible planning, so she was pretty much wearing what she had in Arctic Skavanga: boots, jeans, and the thermal vest she had stripped down to. There was even a heavy parka strapped to her backpack. Great, when what she needed here was a pair of shorts, a flimsy top, and an extra large tub of sunblock.

She wouldn't have had to come if the count had been more reasonable. And was that the real reason, or was this the last-chance saloon for Eva Skavanga as far as men were concerned?

'Meaning?' she flashed out loud, then glanced around guiltily to make sure no one had heard her talking to herself. She really was wound up. Meaning, she reasoned as she plodded on, Count Roman Quisvada threw off the sort of confidence that said he would be very good in in bed… Now she had to take a moment to think about that.

Planting her hands in the small of her back, she was forced to accept that she wouldn't know too much about being good in bed. She wasn't completely innocent. She wasn't exactly experienced, either. She'd had a few fumbles, none of which had encouraged her to try the experience again. She frightened men off. If they weren't limp to begin with, they certainly were by the time she'd finished with them. And then somehow the time for experimenting passed her by. She got too old for it. She missed the boat. She told herself it didn't matter. She just wasn't interested in sex.

Until she met the count.

Allowing her backpack to slide to the ground, she rested her hands on her knees to catch her breath. Lifting her head, she weighed up the gates guarding his lair. They were big, but not so big she couldn't climb over them. Chucking her backpack over first, she followed, scrambling up the ornamental ironwork like a monkey. They'd told her in the village that with the big wedding on it was unlikely that anyone would be home, which was great for her purposes. It gave her a chance to have a snoop around before the count returned.

She quickly spotted some cameras, but no alarms went off. Lots of people had cameras, but very few were switched on, she'd heard. Undeterred, she started to march up the broad, impressive drive. Bottle-green cypress trees stood on parade on either side, providing some welcome shade, while the neatly groomed gravel crunched beneath her feet. The palazzo was framed against a brilliant blue sky, and with its towers and crenellations, the count's island home looked like something from a fairy tale. It certainly wasn't what she had expected. Festoons of purple bougainvillea softened the walls and hung in swags around the windows, while more fringed the top of the impressive front doors. Colour was mostly grey in Skavanga, but here the blaze of colour was a huge assault on her senses—not unpleasant, though the count's home was certainly a confident reflection of his power and wealth.

Even she had to admit his gardens were exquisite. Colour blazed at her from every side, and there was such an amazing variety of planting. How many people must he employ? she wondered as she ran her fingertips across the immaculate white wall. The count probably had homes like this across the world, she concluded, and none of them could mean as much to him as the simple log cabin she shared with her sisters on the shore of a frozen lake. That was where they had taken their holidays for as long as she could remember. There weren't many luxuries, but she didn't care. Thinking about the symbols that defined her, and those that defined the count, she realised they couldn't be more different.

Having reached the entrance, she raised the heavy knocker and rapped forcefully on the door.

Silence.

Shading her eyes, she peered through the window. They hadn't been exaggerating in the village when they said everyone would be at the wedding. The palazzo appeared to be deserted. Untying her neck scarf, she mopped the grit and sweat from her face as she decided what to do next. Maybe there'd be someone round the back…

There wasn't a soul to be seen, but there was a fabulous pool…

'Hello?'

'Hello? Is anyone there?'

The rhythmical chirruping of the cicadas was her only answer. Her gaze returned longingly to the limpid stretch of cool, clear water. She was melting and dead on her feet. Surely, a quick dip in the pool wouldn't hurt anyone?

Dumping her backpack, she stripped off down to her underwear and padding to the edge of the pool, she performed a perfect swallow dive.

Oh…the sensation…the indescribable bliss…

She stayed underwater for a whole length, and then, because the feeling was just so wonderful, she relaxed into an easy freestyle stroke.

'What the hell?'

The roar hit her out of nowhere. Barely recovered from inhaling half the pool, she somehow made it to the side, where she pressed herself against the blue tiles, horribly aware that she was almost naked.

'Eva Skavanga?' the same angry male voice roared.

It was Roman Quisvada! After months of her doing battle with a name, he was standing at the edge of the pool glaring down at her.

'Yes?' she called back, putting some force behind her voice. Clinging to what little dignity remained to her as she choked on a mouthful of chlorinated water, she shot a combative look up.

Dear God, his shirt was open to the waist. She had never seen so many muscles. Her body responded instantly, and without the slightest regard for Eva's feelings. Her nipples tightened. A pulse beat insistently between her legs. Pool water that had only been cool and refreshing was suddenly titillating against her heated skin. The sun beating down on her shoulders was a warm caress instead of a punishment, and the count looked even better than she remembered.

Holding a jacket, slung over his shoulder with his forefinger thrust through the loop, his sharply cut formal trousers clung lovingly to a tight butt and hard-muscled thighs. His shirt was crisp and brilliant white, and he was very big. He was also ridiculously good-looking—if you went for the rugged type. He was ripped. He was tan—

He was madder than hell. She could feel his fury washing over her. And why wouldn't it, when she'd been a thorn in his side for long enough, and now here she was, swimming in his pool? How the hell was she going to get out of this one?

The girl in his pool was the troublemaker, Eva Skavanga? Incredible! The alarm at the palazzo was connected to his phone and had warned him of an intruder. The cameras had shown the shadowy figure of a girl climbing over his gates. Reason had discounted the possibility that it could be anyone he knew, let alone Eva. Thank God his instinct had got him back here fast. 'Get out of my pool now!'

Positioning himself between the slight, pale figure

in the pool and the towels left for him to use, he was determined to make her suffer for this intrusion.

'Could you pass me a towel, please?' she asked as if he were the pool boy at a hotel.

'I said get out!' His voice would have sent grown men scuttling for cover.

Eva just stared at him. 'I heard you the first time,' she flared, 'but I can't—'

'Can't what?' he rapped. 'Can't move? Can't face me? Can't think up an excuse for why you're here?'

Putting her small palms flat on the tiles at the side of the pool, she sprang out lithely. He took in the vibrant, waist-length mermaid hair, the fabulous breasts, the trim figure, long, long legs, and tiny feet.

She stared at him in silence for a moment and then tried to reach past him for a towel.

He stood in her way. 'When I said I didn't have time to meet with you, I meant it, Ms Skavanga. What the hell are you doing on my island uninvited? We have nothing to discuss.'

'That's your opinion. I've come here to change your mind.'

'I wish you luck with that.' The water had made her underwear translucent. It left nothing to his imagination where her naked body was concerned. And as she stood confronting him pool water cascaded down her body, highlighting every line and curve. It was even trickling down the crack in her butt, he noticed as she turned away to grind her jaw and tap her foot. Maybe she'd think twice about wearing such a tiny thong next time she planned to invade a stranger's pool.

'*Please* pass me a towel,' she ground out, turning

back to him. 'They're just behind you,' she informed him, tilting her chin at a combative angle.

She could wait. He knew the expression in his eyes offered no reprieve. Eva stared back at him without blinking. Somehow she managed not to fold her arms across her chest during this standoff, though he suspected she dearly wanted to. She needn't have worried. He wasn't interested.

Seriously?

As he held her gaze with what was supposed to be disinterest, something unique happened inside him: a slight relaxation of his muscles and a fleeting warmth in his empty heart. He pushed the sensation away, but then the desire to laugh, and not in a cruel way, overcame him. She was just so damn cute.

Until she reminded him icily, 'A towel? When you're ready, Count Quisvada.'

'Certainly, Ms Skavanga.' He reached for one without breaking eye contact.

Eva Skavanga didn't have the slightest idea of the effect she was having on him, and long might it remain that way. She was defensive because she thought herself unattractive to men, he concluded. That was why she tried to frighten them off rather than wait for them to push her away. She was a refreshing change. He was used to glamorous, confident women whose sole aim was to insinuate themselves into his life. There was only one thing worse in his opinion, and that was the ambitious parents with a daughter to trade. He was interested in neither option. He would rather live and die a single man than endure some fake arrangement.

'Thank you,' she said grudgingly when he finally gave her a towel.

Failure was not an option for Eva Skavanga, and neither was caution, apparently. He had to admit, he liked her style. Maybe he wouldn't despatch her on the next ferry home, but would keep her here while it suited him. At least while she was here she couldn't cause trouble at the mine, and by the time he did send her home the work that needed to be done would have been completed.

This was not what she had planned. This was not what she had planned at all. Being caught red-handed by the count—swimming in his pool, trespassing on his grounds—confronting the man himself, when she might as well have been naked and he was elegantly clothed. It was hardly the surprise encounter she had envisaged when she set off from Skavanga, but of course that was the one where she seized the initiative, while the count was still reeling from his surprise at seeing her. There wasn't much reeling going on right now.

'So, Ms Skavanga?' he demanded. 'Do you intend to launch a protest at the side of my pool? Or may I continue on into the palazzo, where I can make arrangements for your immediate removal from the island?'

Not reeling. And definitely not in the mood for negotiations. The count was hostile, and embarrassingly unmoved by her all-but-naked body.

'You can't have me removed.'

'I assure you, Ms Skavanga, I can do anything I want to do.'

'But I've come all this way to see you.' And, damn it, her voice was trembling. She hadn't expected him to be so aggressive. She had imagined a man with an aristocratic pedigree would soften for a woman. How wrong could she be? 'Please—'

'Please, would you forgive me breaking in to your home? Or, please don't deport me from the island?' His voice was wholly mocking.

'Both,' she managed, angry at his tone.

'Begging now, Ms Skavanga?'

'Hardly. I'm merely appealing to your better nature.' She raised a brow as she spoke, as if to say she realised now how unlikely it would be that he had one.

He might have expected a trespasser to be mortified to have been caught out, or to beseech him with pleading in her voice, and maybe even a few crocodile tears thrown in, all that was reflected in Eva's face was challenge. So much hung on this meeting with him, according to her, so couldn't she even manage a climb down this time? Of course she couldn't. It wasn't in her nature. And that was half her appeal, he realised. 'You have a very high opinion of yourself, Ms Skavanga.'

For the first time her gaze flickered. It reinforced his opinion that beneath the *braggadocio* she was insecure.

Eva shifted uneasily from foot to foot. In her world she was confident, because people knew her and knew what to expect. She was never intentionally rude to anyone. She was just forceful. At least, that was how she liked to think of it.

Guilt flashed into her mind as she remembered the much-regretted argument with her sister.

And sometimes she was just plain rude, she accepted, but now she must keep the count listening long enough to convince him that the reason she was here overrode anything she might have done to see him. Extracting diamonds from the Skavanga mine at any cost couldn't be right. But his expression suggested she would have to eat some humble pie, or there'd be no discussion.

'I'm sorry,' she managed to grind out. 'I realise we've made a bad start.'

'You have,' he agreed.

CHAPTER THREE

DID THIS MAN get some sort of kick out of humiliating her? Eva wondered as she stood tense and angry by the side of the count's fabulous pool. She might have learned a lesson in where being reckless led, but she wasn't about to back down. 'If it hadn't been for you accelerating work at the mine, I wouldn't be here.'

'Is that what you call recovering the situation, Ms Skavanga? I think you'd better follow me into the house. I'll decide what to do with you when you've had a chance to shower and change into some fresh clothes.'

The last thing she had expected was that he would invite her into his home. 'Thank you,' she managed awkwardly.

'Don't thank me, Ms Skavanga. Just think of yourself as an inconvenience I don't intend to suffer much longer. And when I march you out of here, you stay off my property for good. Is that understood?'

Anger flashed through her as the count turned away and started to walk towards the house. She had to stop herself saying something she'd regret. If her concerns for the drilling hadn't been hanging over her— If the survival of the mine hadn't been largely dependent on this man—

'Do you understand?' he called out.

'Yes,' she fired back, scowling.

'And while you are a guest in my house there will be no door slamming—no temper tantrums of any kind. Do I make myself clear, Ms Skavanga?'

'Perfectly.' He was remembering that time at Britt's wedding when her body had reacted just as violently to him as it was doing now, and because she was so shocked by her response to him she had slammed the door in his face. She'd felt feminine at Britt's wedding for about five minutes, but the count had changed all that. Fairy-tale bridesmaid into dowdy country bumpkin in no time flat.

'Please follow me into the house, Ms Skavanga.'

She could play it tough with the guys back home, because they knew her and she knew them, but the count didn't have the slightest interest in her as a woman, or as a companion. She should be pleased. No. She should be relieved. But being rejected as unfit for purpose wasn't great.

But if that was how it was going to be, she would keep everything on a business footing. Catching up with him at the door, she offered him her hand. 'Eva Skavanga—'

He ignored the gesture.

Swallowing her pride, she tried again. 'I didn't expect for us to—'

'Meet like this?' he interrupted, hostility rippling off him in big, ugly waves. 'Who would?'

Hostile was far too mild a word to describe the count. And, yes, she'd trespassed on his land, but was that a hanging offence? She'd taken a swim in his pool, but so what? What was the big deal? What was riding the count? What was *his* problem?

The count exuded power and menace and sex, in more or less equal quantities, and admittedly that was fascinating, but it was also intimidating and she had shivers running up and down her spine. But at least she had accomplished something, if only the fact that she had tracked him down.

'Well, at least we're standing face to face,' she said as he opened the door to the palazzo.

'Is that meant to be funny, Ms Skavanga?'

'No. It's merely a statement of fact.'

'Well, here's another fact. Your intrusion in my home is not welcome, and as soon as it can be arranged—'

She pre-empted him. 'As soon as we've talked, I'll go.'

'Go where?' he said, standing back to let her go through the doorway. 'You really haven't thought this through, have you? You rushed here to confront me, without any thought at all, because you'll stop at nothing to get your own way at the mine.'

'Do you blame me when you will never agree to see me? I had to come here. You might not care about Skavanga or the people who live there, but I do. All that's at stake for you is your money.'

'So pumping in my money to keep the town and mine alive, saving people's jobs along the way, means nothing to you?'

'You'll just leave us with a desolate site when you've taken what you want.'

'You don't know what you're talking about, Ms Skavanga. Now are you coming inside or not?'

She couldn't risk alienating him. Had she forgotten that?

He led the intruder across his spacious orangerie at a rate of knots. He didn't welcome unexpected visitors to his sanctuary on the island, least of all trouble-making girls with an agenda.

'I'm not a whinger or a troublemaker,' she shouted after him. 'I'm simply concerned about the speed of your drilling programme.'

He stopped dead. 'Do you have an alternative suggestion, Ms Skavanga?'

She almost cannoned into him.

'Maybe…' Her cheeks flushed red when she realised how close she'd come to touching him. 'I don't have an engineering background like you,' she admitted, surprising him with the speed of her recovery. He was also surprised she had done her research. 'I don't have as many academic qualifications, either,' she added, 'but I do have local knowledge.'

And a good degree, he remembered, wondering why she had never used it.

'Let me reassure you, Ms Skavanga, that the finest minds have assembled to make this project a success.'

'The finest minds, maybe,' she agreed, growing heated. 'But no one local is involved at a decision-making level, so you run the risk of applying the wrong criteria to your thinking.'

'What about your sister, Britt?'

'Britt is just a figurehead—a sop to keep the locals quiet.'

He drew back his head to stare at her. 'How sad that you don't know your own sister.'

'I know enough,' she blustered, but there was guilt in her eyes.

'Your sister is an excellent businesswoman. Decisive and clear-thinking, Britt had led the family business in the absence of your parents and her brother, and now she runs the mine for the consortium—'

'I know all that.'

And he knew Eva had lost the mother who might have softened her at a critical age. Reports said that she now liked to think of herself as a frontierswoman, happier under canvas than in a bed. Or, as others described her, the sister who was all balls and belligerence and a crack shot with a gun. Britt worked for the consortium on merit alone, while Eva had positioned herself against them. Eva didn't want things to change, and had made it widely known that she believed the future of Skavanga lay in the type of tourism that would preserve and pay homage to her unique Arctic landscape, rather than mining, which could only scar the land. He believed the two could co-exist.

'Your sister Britt is a lot more valuable to the future of this project than you seem to think. Perhaps you should speak to her.'

Now she looked thoroughly miserable. He'd found her Achilles heel. Eva cared passionately about her family and the mine, more than she cared about herself.

She was reeling, both at the shock meeting with the count and him inviting her into his fabulous home. They had crossed the gracious glass-walled building opening onto the pool, and had entered a grand, light-filled entrance hall, complete with a sweeping marble staircase that housed a grand piano beneath its curve.

The fabulous setting and the fact that she was wearing a towel had really thrown her. This wasn't her debating outfit of choice, and she felt even worse about the fall out with Britt since the count had made a point of talking about her sister. She knew what Britt had achieved at the mine and couldn't have admired her sister more. Why did everything always come out wrong? Why couldn't she control her tongue for once? For the sake of the mine, she had to try to make amends. 'All I'm asking for is the chance to talk to you, and then I'll go.'

A flash of humour lit his eyes. 'Do I have your word on that?'

'The sooner the better, as far as I'm concerned,' she fired back, unsettled by his worldly, mocking stare.

'And what am I supposed to do with you until then?'

'Listen to me?' she suggested, lashing out again before she could stop herself.

'I set the terms, *Ms* Skavanga. I speak. You listen.'

As the count's lazy gaze washed over her, every part of her warmed. However much she resented him and his autocratic ways, her body remained incredibly impressed.

'And now, as much as I have enjoyed talking to you, I have a wedding to get back to. So if you will excuse me, Ms Skavanga?' He moved towards the stairs.

'Don't worry. I'll still be here when you get back.'

'Oh? Will you?'

She watched in fascination as he ran strong, tanned fingers through his thick black hair. The count was fiercely masculine. He had just enough polish to keep him this side of barbarian, but it was a close run thing. All the designer clothes in the world couldn't hide his warrior frame. He'd been born to fight, and it was hard to imagine him in some cosy aristocratic setting—

'Done staring at me, Ms Skavanga?'

She gave a start. She hadn't realised she was examining him quite so intently. And that smile was back on his mocking lips. Her throat dried. She was used to straightforward emotions: black and white. She was not accustomed to this level of sophisticated banter. 'Please don't let me keep you. I'm quite happy to stay here—'

'In the hall?' He gazed around with a sardonic expression curving his firm, sexy mouth. 'I'm sure you are. But if you think for one minute that I'm happy to leave you unattended in my home? I don't think so, Ms Skavanga. You're coming with me.'

'What?' Shock raced through her body at the thought of an evening with the count.

'You're the last person I'd leave alone in my house. Your reputation precedes you, Ms Skavanga. How do I know you won't change the locks while I'm away?'

Mock all you like, but I'm here and I'm not going anywhere. But...if she did go with him, someone might be able to give her a room for the night. 'Fine,' she agreed. 'I'll come down with you when you leave and wait for you in the village.'

'My same concerns apply,' he said. 'I won't risk you upsetting people. You're here and I'm responsible for you, which means I'm not letting you loose on any unsuspecting villagers. You're going to stay close by me where I can keep an eye on you. You're coming with me to the wedding.'

'A wedding?' She laughed. 'Impossible. I don't have anything remotely suitable to wear.'

'Then you will have to improvise. I'm not leaving

you here on your own, and that's final. And I will be leaving the palazzo in half an hour. You need to be ready by then.'

'But if I could find a bed for the night in the village, surely you would prefer that?'

'I wish you joy of your search. Every bed is taken for the wedding, and, as I have no intention of letting you out of my sight, you have no alternative but to stay here for the night.'

'With you?'

'Well, I'm not going anywhere. Of course, you could return home?' The count glanced at his watch. 'If you hurry, you might catch the last ferry.'

'Do you have any idea how hard it has been to track you down so I can express my concerns to you face to face? Do you seriously think I'm going to leave without doing that?'

The count gave her a look. 'That is one option to consider.'

'Not a chance.'

'In that case,' he murmured in a mocking tone, 'my home is your home for the next twenty-four hours, Ms Skavanga. But don't get any ideas.' His voice hardened. 'You leave when I say you leave. And the next item in your diary is a wedding party, and I am never late.'

She flinched at the count's tone. She wasn't used to being talked to like that. *She* drove situations in Skavanga. She did not take instruction. The count's stare was steady and appraising, and not the least bit amused, when she was more accustomed to good-humoured tolerance of her laddish ways.

'Roman Quisvada.'

'I beg your pardon?' She gazed up, bewildered for a moment as he spoke.

'Introductions,' he said. 'As you're coming to stay in my home, I think we should at least be civil to each other.' He took her hand in a firm grip.

The handshake might have lasted no more than a few seconds, but the effect lasted a lot longer.

'Call me Roman,' he murmured, staring down at her.

As in emperor? Conqueror?

The count's stare suggested either description was apt. One thing was sure, Roman Quisvada only accepted one rank, and that was Commander-in-Chief. Where he led others followed. When he spoke others listened. And much as a wolf wouldn't trouble himself about the ants he trod on, she barely registered a blip on his radar.

Were those black eyes laughing at her again? Arrogant man!

Infuriatingly, her body didn't seem to care. There didn't seem to be an insult he could deal her that could stop her wilful body craving him. Or her eyes devouring him, Eva reluctantly conceded. 'Well, I'm glad I've got your interest at last,' she said coolly, checking her towel was securely fixed.

'Oh, you've got my interest,' he confirmed as he started to mount the stairs. 'Though there may come a day when you wish you hadn't.'

'Are you threatening me?' Her voice sounded much smaller than she had intended.

'I'm just letting you know I'll be watching you.'

Her pulse leapt at the thought, while her mind warned her frantically that this was not a good thing. 'That's fine by me,' she said with a careless shrug. 'You can waste your time watching me all you want. I don't know what you think I'm going to do.'

'Right now you're going to take a shower and change your clothes, and then you're going to meet me in the hall.'

She bridled at his orders. And wearing what? A tee bearing the name of an ancient rock band and a fresh pair of jeans? A wedding had been the very last thing on her mind when she left Skavanga, and it certainly wasn't in her nature to insult the bride and groom by turning up wearing something like that. 'I'd much rather wait on the sidelines for you.'

'I'm sure you would. But that's not how it's going to be, Eva. We're going down to the village together, and we're going to attend the wedding together.'

'Won't people ask questions?'

'And if they do?'

'Wouldn't it be easier for you to spare a few minutes to talk to me before you leave for the wedding?' she suggested, trying hard not to register Roman's intoxicating, warm and spicy scent.

'Easy isn't my way, Eva.'

'Well, if a wedding's more important to you—'

'That's enough,' he rapped, shocking her into silence. 'Shall we both examine our motives for being here, Miss Self-Righteous? I'm here on the island for my cousin's wedding. What's your excuse?'

CHAPTER FOUR

THIS MAN DIDN'T just bore out her eyes with his stare. He bore down on her. Physically. Until they were standing just inches apart. Eva tried not to flinch or step back. If she did she'd fall down the stairs. 'You know why I'm here.'

'Do I? Do I, really?' Roman pressed, smiling in a way that chilled her.

'You should do.'

'Should I?'

His experience was so far in advance of hers, she didn't stand a chance. He actually thought there was some other reason for her visit than concern for the mine.

And wasn't there?

'Nothing to say?' he murmured, the light in his eyes making her feel more awkward than ever.

There was a lot she could say, but nothing she was going to share with him. She wasn't used to being pinned down and made to answer. She wasn't used to a man staring into her eyes as if he could read her private thoughts. 'My only reason for being here is Skavanga. I would have thought that was obvious.'

'To you, perhaps,' he said with that same disquieting look. 'Shall we go upstairs, Eva?'

She moved past him into this very different world, and was almost home free when he put out an arm to stop her. 'You have done your research on the mine, haven't you, Eva?'

That compelling gaze was far too close and far too dangerous. 'Of course I have. I grew up with it.'

'Things change over time.' Roman shifted position slightly, making a little more space between them, but also reminding her of how intensely charismatic he was. 'Iron ore and minerals run out, Eva, and without the diamonds the mine is worthless.'

'Britt said the traditional minerals are close to running out. She didn't say they had run out.'

'It's only a matter of time.'

She shook her head—not just to disagree with this, but to break the disturbing eye contact. 'They've been running out for as long as I can remember.'

'And this time it's true.' Roman stepped in front of her so she had to look at him. 'The mine has only survived this long because Britt has been holding it together as well as she has. She kept the truth from you and your sister so you didn't have to worry. But that's not a situation you and I can allow to continue, is it, Eva?'

Oh, he was good. 'Britt doesn't have much choice but to follow the party line now you and the consortium are in control.'

'Your sister is in full agreement with everything we do. Perhaps you should have asked her about that before you left Skavanga.'

Instead of arguing with Britt as she had. Another

wave of guilt washed over her and for once she bit back all the angry words on the tip of her tongue. 'But, honestly, diamonds? Expensive trinkets? Is it really worth ruining the polar landscape for that?'

'You have a lot to learn about diamonds, Eva.'

She remained unconvinced. 'There must be some other way to save the mine.'

'When you find one, let me know. Meanwhile, you're welcome to use one of the guest suites.'

'But we haven't finished talking yet.'

'I have,' Roman said flatly.

And she was in no position to attract a potential landlady while she was dripping wet with a towel wrapped around her.

'You've got twenty minutes, Eva. And then I'm leaving,' he warned as she jogged past him up the stairs

'I'll try not to keep you waiting.'

'Please yourself. I won't wait.'

'Where is this guest suite?' The palazzo was so huge. She turned back to look at him. 'Where do you want me to go?'

Roman's look suggested he'd like to tell her. 'When you get to the top of the stairs, turn left, and take the last door on your right. You can't miss it—it's got a lion's head handle. And hurry up, Eva, I don't have all day.'

'Thank you, Roman.'

Her attempt at meekness earned her a withering look. Lion's head handle. No doubt the handle on his door was a fist.

Building bridges? Not blasting them sky high...

She felt his gaze following her as she ran up the stairs. Roman was so confident in his masculinity he made her feel awkward and inexperienced, as if all her past failed encounters with men were an open book to him. No doubt he was having a good laugh at her expense. She had left it too long to risk intimacy with a man. She didn't like to do anything unless she did it well, and intimacy was one skill she didn't possess.

'Don't look so worried, Eva.'

She gasped as he bounded in front of her, taking the stairs two at a time.

'You couldn't be safer than you are with me.'

His voice was deep and husky and vaguely amused. He did sense her embarrassment, and he was laughing at her.

So let him. She shrugged as she reached the landing. 'I don't know what makes you think I'm worried. I can handle myself.'

'So I hear,' he said dryly.

She hated herself for reacting so violently. All the tiny hairs on the back of her neck lifted, and heat pulsed insistently through her veins. The power emanating from him flowed around her, embracing her whether she liked it or not. Her sisters would be amazed to see her shaken like this—when they'd stopped laughing. What was so special about tall, dark and perfect, anyway? Why was her body insisting on behaving like this? Roman was so not her type. He was autocratic and overbearing. He was the most insufferable man she'd ever met.

And the most attractive.

He showed no interest in her as a woman, which was a relief. An absolute relief. But it wasn't normal. He could at least pretend. That would be the polite thing to do. And weren't aristocrats supposed to be courteous? Weren't they all raised to behave differently from other people by ferocious nannies with thick rulebooks on how to behave?

'Turn left, I said,' he called out to her.

I knew that. She casually retraced her steps, vowing to keep her thoughts restricted to what she had to do—which did not include fixating on Roman Quisvada.

She checked each door down the long and airy corridor, longing to be safe behind one of them, and away from him, so she could calm down and cool off. Roman had disappeared somewhere in the opposite direction. Good. She'd had enough of Count Roman Quisvada and his sardonic face to last her a lifetime. But look at it this way: she only had to get through tonight at the wedding party. She would just have to bite her tongue.

So long as she didn't bite anything else, that should work.

He groaned with pleasure beneath an ice-cold shower. To his overheated skin the freezing water felt like soothing balm. His senses were heated thanks to Eva. She infuriated him. She attracted him, and that was distracting. There was unfinished business between them. Strength and fire had been his first impression of her at her sister's wedding. His impression of her hadn't changed, but Eva was more complex than he had first thought. She was elusive and thoughtful, passionate, and doggedly determined. And he had always liked a challenge. Eva Skavanga needed taming or she would continue to plague his mind.

Quitting the shower, he grabbed a towel and rang one of his trusted aides in Skavanga. He needed more detail about her.

'Mark? I need a briefing. Yes. Eva Skavanga. She's

here. What do you mean you knew that? Why on earth didn't you tell me?'

He listened to some rambling excuse and quickly realised that young Mark had fallen under Eva's spell. 'Well, now we both know.' He cut his aide off impatiently. 'Yes, of course she's all right. Which brings me to my next question. You seem to be an admirer of this woman. Why? She seems to me to be more trouble than she's worth?'

'Don't write her off,' Mark advised. 'Eva's a hothead and likes to think she's one of the boys, but she's got a heart of gold—too trusting, maybe.'

'Not in my case.'

Mark ignored this. 'She has her heart set on eco-tourism saving Skavanga. She's terrified that our mining project will reduce the town to a smoking pile of steel, with panhandlers drinking in the streets and plastic tables and plastic food replacing the cultural traditions of her Arctic home.' This much Roman already knew.

His young aide was besotted. The thought almost made him veer away from asking the question uppermost in his mind. 'Didn't you explain that our work will cause minimal upheaval, and that any damage done will be repaired?' And that wasn't all of it.

Mark laughed in an admiring way as his mind turned to a woman it was clear they were both interested in. 'Have you tried reasoning with Eva?'

'Enough.' His voice came out a roar. So much for subtlety. 'Tell me about her relationships.'

There was a silence as Mark considered this. 'There are none,' he said at last on what sounded like a very dry throat.

'Why is that?' He didn't let up the pressure. His hand tightened on the phone. 'She's an attractive woman...'

'Who has half the men of the Arctic Circle racing each other to the South Pole, rather than tangle with her.'

'I thought they bred them tough at the North Pole.'

'They do, but Eva Skavanga is a special case.'

'She has a problem with men?'

'She has an unfortunate attitude with men.'

Mark was being careful with his choice of words. 'Explain,' he insisted.

'The older sister you know—Britt is confident and a great businesswoman. She's self-confident, decisive and married now. The younger girl, Leila, is a bit of an unknown quantity, because she's always been overshadowed by Britt and Eva—'

'Eva's reputation?' he pressed. 'I'm not interested in the other two. They're not out here. She is.'

'Eva's a loner. Maybe she's been hurt at some time.'

'But not so hurt and broken she couldn't turn up here, break into my house and swim in my pool—'

'She broke into your house?'

Now Mark did sound shocked. 'She terrorised me,' Roman said dryly. 'Until I agreed to speak to her about her beloved Skavanga.'

'That sounds like Eva.'

Mark's voice held the same note of admiration that had annoyed him the first time round and that now made him snarl, 'That's enough, Mark. She's a nuisance at best. Forget I even rang you. I'll sort her out. And I'll get rid of her.'

There was a long pause, and then Mark said, 'She's staying with you?'

'Don't worry. She's not my type. I'm taking her to the wedding, and that's all.'

'You're taking her to the wedding?'

'Did I employ a parrot? I'm taking her so I can keep an eye on her.'

As Mark gave a nervous laugh Roman guessed his young aide was in no way reassured as to the immediate fate of one Eva Skavanga. 'Relax, Mark. I have no immediate plans for her.' Later perhaps, he mused.

'If you had allowed me to put her through to you when you were in Skavanga I guess she wouldn't have made the trip.'

'You sound worried, Mark. Whose side are you on?'

'Yours, of course,' Mark protested, 'but—'

'I didn't avoid Eva's earlier requests to see me. I ignored them. You should know by now that misguided pleas from emotional women cut no ice with me. Eva's a small shareholder with no special privileges just because she happens to be a member of the family that gave its name to the mine. I'll treat her the same as any other small investor, no better no worse.'

But on a personal front?

Taming Eva Skavanga held considerable appeal.

He ended the call, having found out what he wanted to know. Eva was unattached. And doubly intriguing. His thoughts turned to having her passion pinned beneath him. He shrugged and smiled faintly as he ditched the towel. There were sound business reasons for keeping her close. While she was here she couldn't disrupt work at the mine. Any damage caused by the drilling would be made good, which Eva would have known if she had attended the meetings he'd held in Skavanga instead of picketing them. Now she was trapped on an island with a ferry that operated at his command and he'd send her home when it suited him.

Slinging on a pair of chinos and a clean shirt, he thought about shaving then parked the idea. As an image of Eva's body flashed into his mind he reached into a cupboard to find a bottle of suncream. This was no godly act on his part. She lived in the Arctic and the sun was strong here. He didn't want her too sore to have sex with. Giving his thick black hair one final run-through, he glanced in the mirror and imagined Eva's defiant face glaring back at him. If there was anything he enjoyed more than a tussle with a hot-blooded woman, he couldn't think what it was. Eva would be his guest at the wedding, and then, just as she had requested, he would give her his undivided attention.

She had found the door with the lion's head handle. Thank goodness. This place was like a city. The door was heavy, silky cream, and as she closed her hand around the lion's head it was a surprising degree of pleasure. Would everything be so tactile here? *Including the count?*

Stop with the fantasies. She had around fifteen minutes to shower, change and meet him downstairs. All of which might have been fine if she could only stop gazing round like a country yokel. She had opened a door onto a wonderland of art and luxury, functionality and extravagance combined. Like the rest of the palazzo, the decor was discreet yet obviously expensive. Taupe, ecru, ivory and chalky-white, with a couple of showpiece ornaments and a huge unframed painting, picked up the tints of the throw on the bed—

Okay…that unframed piece? The homage to Picasso?

On closer inspection she discovered it was a Picasso. The last time she'd seen the painting it had been hanging in a gallery in Stockholm, labelled 'on loan' from an unnamed benefactor.

Roman Quisvada lived in quite some style. And grudgingly, she had to admit she liked it. It did surprise her that such a powerful brute of a man lived like this in the home of a discerning connoisseur. The count was an interesting man—in more ways than one.

Dropping her backpack on what was probably an extremely expensive rug, she tried not to draw unnecessary comparisons between the count's seductive lifestyle and the seductive count. She scrunched her toes appreciatively in the soft wool as she crossed the room to inspect the balcony overlooking the placid azure sea. The scent of blossom was heavy and intoxicating, and she wished she could remain dreaming a little longer as she leaned over the stone balustrades, but the clock was ticking and she still had to shower and dress.

Four doors faced her in the room. The first turned out to be a dressing room, for the guest who had everything, and who was only used to the best. Not Eva Skavanga, that was for sure. The second door revealed a gym. The third, a marble-lined bathroom. Her jaw dropped. And stuck. With its sunken bath and shower big enough for two, the bathroom could best be described as sumptuous. There were enough white fluffy towels for an army, and the water pressure was fierce enough to fill a lake. She wandered back into the bedroom, where she couldn't resist a few bounces on the mega-sized bed where inviting crisp white sheets still held the faint scent of sunshine, and the throw, with its tints echoing those of the fabulous painting on the wall, reminded her of a fading summer sky. How was she ever going to drag herself away from this?

A sharp rap on the door gave her that answer.

'Eva?'

She hadn't even showered yet! 'Five minutes?' she yelled back.

'Not a minute more.' Roman sounded less than amused.

How would he punish her if she was late?

She absolutely had to stop thinking like that. Even as a joke! She might forget herself and come on to him. She could act tough back in Skavanga, but she was playing well out of her league here.

Drying off after her shower, she twisted her hair into a messy up-do on top of her head, securing it with the single hairclip she had retrieved from the bottom of her pack. It was just a boring old plastic thing that came in a pack of six, but there was no time to dry her hair properly. And right on cue the hammering on the door started again. If she left Roman hanging much longer he'd crash the room.

She was a campaigner not a stylist, so what was she worried about? Eva thought as she viewed her reflection in the cheval mirror in the bedroom. So what if Roman was clad in the finest couture, while the best that could be said for her was that she was clad? He'd asked for this. She wasn't a fashion guru, either.

'Ready.' Buoyed with renewed confidence, she flung the door wide.

'No.'

'No?'

'No,' he repeated flatly.

She had been on the point of apologising for her casual appearance, but now she was stoked. Her cheeks blazed red as he stared at her.

'You can't go to the wedding dressed like that.'

'Well, what do you suggest?'

What made things worse was the sight of Roman dressed for the wedding. Wearing chinos, cinched with a beautifully tooled leather belt, he had a pale linen jacket slung over his shoulders and a dark shirt underneath. He looked even more amazing than before if such a thing were possible. His thick dark hair was still damp from the shower, and stubble was already shading his disapproving face. It should be illegal to look so hot. If every ruthless entrepreneur looked like Roman Quisvada, it was no wonder they could strip assets faster than Eva could throw a spanner in their works.

'Well?' she prompted as he continued to narrow his eyes and ponder. 'I didn't come here planning to attend a wedding. I don't even want to go. You suggested it—'

'Yes, I did,' he admitted thoughtfully.

'Are you ashamed of me?'

He seemed to come round, as if this genuinely hadn't occurred to him.

'I have no feelings regarding you at all. I just think you might feel more comfortable if you were dressed differently, that's all.'

'That settles it,' she flashed, backing into the room. 'I'll wait for you in the village—'

With whip-fast reactions, he held the door firm.

'Wait for me where?' He stood belligerently in her way. 'You'll come with me—and you'll come with me now. This isn't a multiple-choice, Eva. The decision has already been made.'

CHAPTER FIVE

'DO YOU SERIOUSLY think anyone will notice what I'm wearing?' she said, starting to worry.

'*Everyone* will notice what you're wearing.'

'Because I'm with you,' she scoffed.

'They'll be curious,' Roman admitted with a shrug.

I bet they will. 'Why don't you just say I'm an employee who turned up unexpectedly?'

For the first time he seemed amused. 'No one will believe that, Eva. They know me too well to think I could be surprised that way.'

'Because all your employees do what you tell them, I suppose.'

He gave her a sleepy look that suggested everyone did as he told them—with one notable exception. 'Maybe they'll think I'm a roadie with the band?' Lifting her shoulders, she let them drop again.

'Is that what you want people to think?' Roman's lips pressed down attractively.

'I don't care what they think—'

'But I think you do,' he said. 'These are good people, Eva. I think you'll want them to like you.'

That was the one answer she hadn't expected—the one answer she didn't have a smart retort for. Concern from Roman was so unexpected that, quite inappropriately, her eyes filled with tears. She wasn't used to people other than her sisters showing concern for her. They were generally afraid to in case she bit their head off. She had never been so wrong-footed before. And had never felt quite so out of place.

'I'm just trying to be practical, Eva,' Roman pointed out. 'I'm trying to help you. Why can't you accept that? And we don't have much time.'

As he glanced at his watch she knew he was right. It would be rude if the one man who was surely a valued guest arrived late at the party. 'So what do you suggest?' she said, shrugging unhappily.

'That belt,' he murmured.

'What belt?' she said, frowning impatiently.

'The one you're wearing on your jeans. It's very pretty.'

She was surprised he'd noticed. It was a good belt. She'd bought it when she had bought a few things in memory of her mother who had been über feminine. It was just a slim leather belt inlaid with polished turquoise set in silver.

The belt was giving him a welcome distraction from the sight of Eva's spectacular breasts pressing against her too-tight top. They were just one more attribute she seemed totally oblivious to. The belt had given him an idea. Yes, he could do without attending his cousin's wedding with the complication of such an unconventional 'plus one', but as she was going, and as, contrary to Eva's opinion of him, he wasn't in the habit of humiliating people, he wanted to help her out.

'Where are you going?' she called after him as he backed off and strode away down the corridor.

He had never found a good enough reason to explain himself.

He was back in a few short seconds with a new white tee still in its packet.

'What am I supposed to do with that?' she said as he handed it over.

'You're supposed to go back inside your room and put it on.'

Taking it out of the wrapping, she shook it out. 'Are you joking? This will drop straight off me. I'm guessing it's yours. You're twice my size, Roman.'

'At least twice.'

'So…?'

'So just put it on for me. If it doesn't work, we'll park the idea. Just try it,' he coaxed, masking a grin at her expression. 'You never know. You might like the look.'

'I very much doubt it.'

'Just do it, Eva, or we'll be late.' His tone had changed, and with a mutinous look she retreated behind the door, slamming it, for the second time in their short acquaintance, in his face.

Pride vied with her natural caution, but eventually practicality won the day. Roman was right. She didn't want to look like a complete idiot at the party, and at least if she tried to make a dress out of his top she wouldn't look so wildly out of place. It was a party on a beach. She'd give it a try, anyway. Why not?

The tee did not fit.

Of course it didn't fit. Why had she ever thought it would? Twisting her hair, like her temper, into an even tighter knot of fury, she opened the door.

'Problem?' Roman murmured, easing away from the wall.

Apart from the fact that her hair was half falling down, while the tee had no such inhibitions and would have dropped straight off if she hadn't grabbed hold of it.

'No. No problem. I always go out for the night dressed like this.' She garnished the denial with a withering look.

Did he have to look quite so relaxed…so hot, so amused?

'The problem is glaringly obvious. The top gapes everywhere. What do you imagine will happen if I let go?'

'I'd rather not imagine.' But the sexy mouth tugged as Roman slouched on one hip. 'I think you need help.'

'Is that meant to be funny?'

'You're so touchy. Do you have a guilty conscience, Eva Skavanga?'

'Why?'

'Maybe you shouldn't have come here after all.'

'And maybe I shouldn't have trusted you to give me a bed for the night as you promised. I had no idea there'd be so many complications.'

'Come here.'

'I will not.' She backed away as he beckoned to her.

'Eva…'

His voice was soft.

Like a lion tamer hiding the whip. She retreated another step. She didn't like that look on his face one bit. She almost shot out of her skin when he put his hands on her shoulders. The knack was to remain calm, she told herself firmly. Don't react. Look him in the eyes. She tottered round stiffly as he slowly turned her in front of him. 'What the hell?'

'Where's the belt, Eva?'

'The belt? I left it with my jeans. And if you're thinking what I think you're thinking, I can tell you now that a belt isn't going to save this situation.'

'Just get it, will you, and let me be the judge of that?'

Another order? She huffed and narrowed her eyes. But, hey, what harm did it do to go get the belt? At least she could prove him wrong.

He fastened the belt loosely round her waist.

'Almost there,' he murmured, slipping the neck of the tee off one shoulder.

She tried not to flinch when his hand brushed her neck, but a shiver ran through her as he brushed her naked flesh.

He stood back to take a look. 'Just one more tweak—'

She gasped as he released her messy hair, allowing it to cascade in wild abandon around her shoulders.

'Now look what you've done.' She pulled a face as she tried to scrape her hair back.

'Bellissima...' Roman moved her hand away. 'Now you're ready.'

She swung away from him in fury. And caught sight of herself in the mirror. Goodness. She looked almost feminine.

'From temperamental tomboy to pale, Botticelli waif,' Roman observed with the irony back in his voice. 'I've no doubt you'll be the toast of the party.'

He'd be toast if he tried anything like that again. 'I very much doubt it,' she scoffed. 'And if you're trying to suggest that I look anything like Botticelli's painting of the Birth of Venus—I'm not naked. And I've certainly no intention of standing in a shell.'

'Just make sure you don't stand *on* one when you're

down on the beach,' he said, not the least bit fazed by her heated expression.

More mockery. More...everything. Wicked eyes... Fabulous teeth...Bad, *bad* sexy mouth.

'Are you ready, Eva?'

For anything. 'If you say so,' she conceded grudgingly, somehow managing to drag her gaze away.

She pointedly ignored Roman's offer to hook her arm through his and walked past him. 'Thank you so much for helping me to style my outfit... It's almost impossible to find a good stylist these days.'

'Don't push it, *signorina*,' he growled somewhere far too close behind her.

Her spine tingled at his proximity, but if Roman Quisvada happened to be lifting one of his arrogant ebony brows right now, he could stick his courtly airs and graces where the sun didn't—

'You look great,' he said, catching up with her easily, and matching his stroll to her purposeful stalk towards the stairs.

'Thank you,' she managed tightly. Her voice was about the only thing that was tight. Unfortunately for her, Roman gave great sensation in places she normally didn't waste much time thinking about. Would blanking sensation even be possible with this man? To distract herself she fell back a few paces to see what all the fuss was about. Apart from obviously looking amazing, Roman Quisvada exuded confidence and moved with the ease of an athlete. He wore his thick, wavy black hair long, which she liked, especially when it was still damp and wavy from the shower—

'Keep up, Eva. I don't want to be late.'

She pulled a face behind his back as he started across

the hall, but not before her senses had registered the curve of his sensual mouth as he turned his head to issue this instruction. He was certainly one arrogant piece of work. She had never encountered anyone like Roman Quisvada before—

'Eva,' he rapped, swinging the front door wide.

Did he have to stand waiting for her with his thumb tucked inside his belt with his long lean fingers directing her gaze to the main attraction?

'Shall we?' he invited mockingly.

Not if I can help it, she thought, having taken in the size of the attraction.

By the time they reached the beach it was already packed with party guests. Roman was greeted like returning royalty. Which was great for Roman and a whole new experience for Eva—especially the compliments she received from the men. Not for the first time since she landed in Italy, she was glad she spoke the language. It wouldn't have been half so much fun if she hadn't understood all their chat.

'I feel like Cinderella at the ball,' she admitted, hot-faced after the latest round of attention from a hunting pack of Roman's male friends.

He didn't seem too impressed. 'My friends find you...intriguing.'

'Because they haven't seen me before?' she guessed. 'Or because they wonder what I'm doing with you?'

'Neither. You're attractive and they're hot-blooded men with a healthy interest in attractive women.'

Attractive? *She* was attractive? That was news to her. And it was the first time any man had said that about her in her hearing. Stubborn. Argumentative. Competitive. Tempestuous. Or just plain stroppy—these were all labels she was familiar with. Could the 'attractive' label account for the black look Roman was giving his friends?

Really?

She wanted to smile.

'Something amusing you?' he said, turning back to her, frowning deeply.

'No,' she said, acting surprised. Seeing his face, she could almost believe Roman was jealous. That probably didn't sound like much to a normal woman, but it was certainly unique in Eva's experience. Men shied away from her in Skavanga, unless she was dressed in jeans and giving them a hard time, while here in the Med they flocked around. And, actually, she was quite enjoying it, especially as she knew she was at absolutely no risk at all—not from Roman and not from his friends. At least, not while he was around. Roman had made it quite clear that he was leader of the pack and no one trespassed on his territory.

As Roman chatted to some more guests who eyed her up speculatively, she toyed with the pretty belt and thought of her mother. Utta Skavanga had made no secret of the fact that she despaired of Eva ever developing feminine traits. And the harder she'd tried to instil her femininity in Eva, the more Eva had rebelled. She'd felt a failure compared to her beautiful sisters, and had chosen to become a tomboy instead. The tomboy she still was today.

Correction: the tomboy she had been until today. Trust an Italian to breathe life into that side of her. Roman's innate flair had brought his friends flocking around.

'Your friends are nice,' she said when he turned back to her.

'Nice?' he queried, turning to see some of the men were still staring at Eva. 'They're unscrupulous villains, every one of them.'

She had to hide a smile seeing Roman glowering. Maybe he did care a little bit—

And now she was being ridiculous. Roman was a hot-blooded Mediterranean man, interested in every woman with breath in her body, because that was his default setting. But it was good to have his interest, if only for one night. It was new and different for her. And not unpleasant. Men generally showed an interest when they wanted her to change a tyre, so they didn't get their suits dirty, or maybe to operate a heavy-lifting machine down the mine if someone wanted to go home early. Apart from that, her encounters with the opposite sex had been restricted to darts practice, snooker matches, and keeping score ringside at the gym, none of which exactly offered an opportunity to flex her femininity muscle.

'And you didn't need to be quite so friendly,' Roman added, turning to give her all his attention.

'And why do you care?' she said, giving him the cold eye.

She waited in vain for some flattery.

'I don't care.'

'Well, you could have fooled me.'

'You look cute in that outfit. Dangerously cute.'

'Oh, please! Cute? Pass the sick bucket, will you?' She was transported back down the mine, jousting with the men. She was so sure Roman was mocking her, she had to hit back first. And, for goodness' sake! Belligerent, laddish, abrasive, any of those adjectives would suit her. But *cute*?

'If you don't believe me, just look at yourself,' he said, turning her to face the bar.

There was a long mirror behind the counter and in between the bottles and darting bartenders Eva could see the reflection of a girl she hardly recognised—a girl with flushed cheeks and bright eyes, and a wild tumble of glittering copper hair—a slim girl standing next to a colossus who looked like every woman's dream. But instead of feeling thrilled or flattered, she felt her stomach clench with apprehension. The old Eva was back and ready to defend against hurt and ridicule, and against all those things Eva had never quite got the hang of, like accepting a genuine compliment with a simple 'thank you'.

'If I'd had anything else to wear, I'd have worn it,' she flashed ungraciously.

Roman's lips twitched suspiciously.

'Are you laughing at me? Did I say something funny?'

She was totally out of her comfort zone, feeling increasingly hot and awkward. She couldn't compete with the other girls at the party with their sleek, immaculately groomed hair and their expensive designer gowns. She should have known Roman would end up teasing her. It was probably the only reason he had invited her to the party. It was probably his way of punishing her for causing disruption at the mine and for arriving on his island uninvited—

'Where do you think you're going?'

He caught hold of her arm as she stormed away.

'I'm going back to the palazzo—'

'Oh, no, you're not,' he said. You're staying here with me. You don't seriously think I'd let you loose on my home, do you?'

'One of your homes—'

'Don't get bogged down in detail,' he snarled, drawing her close.

Roman's eyes were so dark and compelling. He radiated power. She tried to subdue the urge to wriggle away from him so she could bolt as far and as fast as she could. Lifting her chin, she matched his stare. 'I'll stay at the party and play my part.'

She would stay on his island until they had that talk. Let them see how cute he thought her then.

'Excellent,' he said coldly.

She relaxed and stopped fighting him, and he let her go.

With no option but to stay at his side, she began to notice how popular he was—revered even. Why were some of the older people kissing his hand? He was chatting to them like old friends. It was such a warm village, family oriented. That was what she was missing. And it was all her fault. She had worn her family out with her tantrums. She had chosen the wilderness and the wildlife that lived there over them. No one had been able to answer the emptiness inside her when she lost her ma and fa, and only the mighty Arctic landscape seemed to dull the pain. Spending time with people like this only proved how much she took her sisters for granted. When was the last time she had given much thought to the blessings of family life, or swallowed her pride to apologise after a row, which she normally started?

'You're seeing another side of life, I think,' Roman said with his usual perception. 'You appeared to be enjoying yourself and now you've gone all serious again.' He stared at her keenly.

'I'm having a lovely time,' she admitted, 'though I'm curious as to why everyone makes such a fuss of you.'

'My good points are buried so deep you can't see past my disreputable appearance?' he suggested with amusement.

She opened her eyes wide. 'Do you mean you have some good points? What I really want to know,' she said, changing tack, 'is why do some of the older villagers kiss your hand?'

'Would you rather they spat in my eye?'

She rolled her eyes, knowing she wasn't going to get anywhere like this. 'I'm just curious, that's all.'

And Roman's look said she could remain that way.

CHAPTER SIX

HE'D SEEN THE looks the old ladies in the village were giving him. He knew they were impatient for him to find a bride. They still thought of him as the rightful heir, the son of the Don who always would be their leader. He wasn't that son, and the business his cousin now ran was wholly legitimate, but the elders of the village still looked to Roman to care for them and to provide them with an heir. He did care for them, and he would always protect them, but sadly he had to disappoint them where attending tonight's party with an attractive stranger was concerned.

It was ironic to think he used to resent this tight-knit community, believing he could never be part of it, and yet he now felt at the heart of it. But then his confident belief in who he was and where he belonged had been shattered on his fourteenth birthday—

'Roman?'

'My apologies, Eva, I was distracted for a moment.'

'Please don't let me disturb you.' She was being sarcastic, he gathered as she added, 'I'm quite happy scowling and staring into space too.'

He matched her look with one of his own. 'Why don't I introduce you to some more people?'

'Get me off your hands?' she suggested.

'Oh, no. I'll be close by, watching you.'

'Great.' As promised, she scowled.

This was a unique event for him. He was used to women who knew where they stood and what they wanted, and who went straight for his jugular. They made no call on his emotions, and up to now he hadn't wanted them to. Their interest in his body and his bank balance had always been enough for him, but Eva really wound him up. He might even say some long-forgotten protective instinct had kicked in when his friends had clustered round.

Eva thought she knew what she wanted, but she didn't have a clue. Her body language told him one thing, while her worried eyes told him something else. She looked sensational, but hardly seemed aware of the admiring glances she was getting. All the men wanted to sleep with her, but took it for granted he was already there.

He hadn't felt anything remotely like this since he had screwed up his youth and vowed never to have feelings again. Caring was a pointless waste of energy, he had decided at age fourteen. And feelings hurt like hell. He had softened since then, but doubted the shame of returning home to his adoptive parents after being shunned by his blood family would ever leave him. After the love and care his adoptive parents had given him, he had betrayed them in the most terrible way. *And for what?*

'You're doing it again,' Eva exclaimed, jolting him back to the present. 'Only this time I suppose I should be glad you don't have a weapon to hand.'

'What do you mean?' He knew, and shrugged the bad mood away.

'We should enjoy the party, now we're here,' she pointed out.

'You're stealing my lines.'

They almost smiled at each other.

The moment passed. He controlled himself and relaxed. Eva had caused him more than enough trouble in Skavanga, but beneath the bluster he could see now that she was just a shy, awkward girl, out of her comfort zone, trying to do the best she could for other people. In that they weren't so different. And whatever else he thought about Eva Skavanga, he had to admire her pluck. They should forget their differences tonight and see where that took them. To smooth the path, he led her towards more familiar territory. 'Tell me something about your family,' he suggested.

'Why do you want to know?' She stared at him suspiciously.

He didn't blame her for being wary. He hadn't exactly welcomed her onto the island, and now he expected her to expose the people closest to her.

It was too much too soon and, as he suspected she would, she quickly changed the subject.

Roman's mood swings confused her. For a moment when his eyes had darkened, the strength of his unspoken feelings had frightened her. But some sixth sense had reassured her that those feelings had something to do with his past. Even so, it was a relief when some more people stopped by to chat with him and the spotlight moved off her. She didn't want to share her feelings with him. She didn't want to talk about her family to a man she didn't know. She hadn't planned on giving Roman Quisvada any sort of insight into who she was or what made her tick. She still didn't. But she did have to admit that watching him talking to other people was an eye-opener. He seemed genuinely interested in everything they had to say, and part of her wished she could let him in just a little bit. He was engaged and animated, and obviously someone that the people here were glad to call their friend. She envied his easy way with people. She'd never had that knack.

'Eva, I'd like to introduce you to—'

In fairness, Roman introduced her round as if she were a valued visitor, rather than a pain in the neck he would be only too pleased to throw off the island. Everyone made her feel welcome. Maybe she'd never given people a chance before, imagining she would be ignored or passed over for someone more interesting.

Roman had a real talent for bringing people together, she realised as one of the women called back to her, 'Come and see us again soon, Eva,' as her family closed around her to take her off to supper.

'Oh, yes, please do come back again soon, Eva,' Roman said with maximum irony.

'You can cut out the mocking right now,' she said, giving him one of her looks. 'Or I will come back. I promise you that.'

He surprised her with a laugh, though they both knew it would be a cold night in hell before that happened.

'So… Your family,' he said.

Did this man ever give up?

'You have two sisters, Britt and Leila, and a brother, Tyr. Your parents are dead, as are mine.'

She was all for changing the subject pronto, but as a shadow crossed Roman's face her better self kicked in. 'I'm sorry for your loss,' she said quietly.

'And I for yours. It must have been hard for you when your parents were killed.'

'My sisters were wonderful—Tyr was too, but it's always hard to lose a parent.' Why this sudden urge to reach out to him?

How could she not when Roman's eyes showed the same loss she felt? Eva reasoned. The pain was something she never showed the world, but she guessed it must have been in her eyes too, because for once neither of them came up with a smart retort. In fact, just for a moment there was a real connection between them.

'You don't know where Tyr is, then?' Roman broke the spell first.

'He's off doing whatever it is Tyr does.' She felt a pang of loss for the brother who had been gone too long. 'Tyr left home after our mother's funeral and hasn't been seen since.'

'You're smiling.'

'Just remembering the riotous holidays when we were younger. Tyr's idea of fun was skating on the frozen lake to see who fell in first.'

'Risky but happy times,' Roman guessed.

'Yeah…' She grew thoughtful, remembering that was before the mine had started failing and their father had turned to drink.

'You okay, Eva?'

Roman was frowning. She refocused, realising he was concerned. To be truthful, she wasn't sure if she was okay or not. A sense of loss had just hit her like a sledgehammer. Perhaps that was because the families here had made her realise she couldn't keep living in the past, and the way she was heading she would never build a future.

She was let off the hook again by more people stopping by to talk to Roman. Laughing sloe-eyed *signorinas* flirted with him, while ridiculously good-looking men slapped him on the back. He had a good word for everyone—until one of the young men asked her to dance. For a moment she thought he might explode, but then he pulled back and shrugged as if to say, Good luck to you.

Good luck to her, or to the young man? Either way, having Roman's stare on her back as she moved onto the dance floor was disconcerting, to say the least.

She was tense, but the youth kept a sensible distance between them. In deference to Roman, she suspected as he threw a glance through a gap in the crowd on the dance floor as if to reassure the count that he was taking good care of his companion. Roman was at the bar with friends, but every now and then she could still feel his stare. The youth was giving knowing glances to his friends as if to say: Have you seen who I'm dancing with? Yes. That's right. The girl who came to the party with the count. So at worst she was a nuisance, and at best she was a meaningless trophy to a boy who hardly needed to shave.

Perfect.

And just an hour or so ago she had imagined she would be the wallflower while Roman and his friends had fun. The irony of it was, she was having a good time with great people, while the one person she wanted to spend time with couldn't give a damn.

* * *

His blood was racing through his veins, pounding in his temple, threatening to provoke him into the type of action he abhorred at weddings. Initially, he had been glad when one of the village youths—a polite lad from a good family well known to him—had invited Eva onto the dance floor. He had tried telling himself that he deserved a break from the redhead, and that he had done his duty by her. And, as they had agreed, now she was here there was no reason why she shouldn't enjoy the party. But he had not expected to feel like this—as if he couldn't bear to let her out of his sight for one second, or that he had to keep on checking where the boy's hands were. A mere matter of millimetres could turn him from heated into a raging bull. Making his excuses, he left his friends.

She was enjoying herself—having a wonderful time, Eva told herself firmly. Why wouldn't she when she was dancing with her feet in the surf on a sugar-sand beach? The youth was polite enough. She couldn't fault him. Even the fact that he was only dancing with her to impress his friends didn't help. Nothing helped.

She tried again. This. Was Great. Dancing in the moonlight on an exotic beach? What could be better?

Dancing with Roman.

She glanced at the bar, wondering where he was, and had to remind herself that they weren't really a couple. They weren't a couple at all. He had no claim on her. She had no claim on him. And she didn't want to appear rude. Everyone was being so kind to her at the party, even this enthusiastic youth. She owed it to him to finish the dance. But why did she feel as if everything had gone flat? The setting was incredible. The sky was a piece of black velvet studded with diamond stars with just enough scudding pewter clouds to add some drama. The music was beguiling, and the scent of food was making her mouth water…

'That food smells wonderful.' She politely removed herself from the young man's arms. 'I'm absolutely starving, aren't you?'

'Would you like me to get you something to eat, *signorina*?'

'Oh, no, that's okay. I don't want to keep you from your friends.'

The youth was off like a hare from the traps. Eva smiled ruefully, knowing she was just a game to him. She was just a game to Roman too… She looked around, trying to find him, and came up blank. Never mind, she'd get something to eat. Chefs in tall white hats had been working tirelessly on several barbecues all night. She chose a giant-sized baguette with all the trimmings, and it was only when she bit into it that she realised how hungry she was. When had she last eaten?

'I see you've finished dancing.'

'Roman? Sorry…' She swung around and almost choked. 'You startled me.'

'So I see. You'd better wash that down,' he said as he offered her an ice-cold misted bottle.

The sharp tang of homemade lemonade made her cough and splutter even more. This was hardly the role she had written for herself back in Skavanga—the role featuring a confident heroine who knew exactly what her mission was, and how to achieve success. In that version of events she would be forthright and concise.

She would be dignified and compelling. She would not be choking on a sausage sandwich.

She tried hard not to notice that Roman was barefoot with his chinos rolled up, or that he had the most incredibly powerful calves. He'd been wading in the surf, judging by the spray covering his clothes. And she was paying him a great deal too much attention. And in all the wrong places, she realised, lifting her chin to meet his mocking gaze.

'I hope you're having a good time?' His face was deeply shadowed as he asked the question.

How could she not? She would have to be wood from the neck up not to lap up this sort of encounter. It was scary. It was exciting. It was so much more than she had ever dreamed it could be. Moonlight made everyone more mysterious, and Roman Quisvada by moonlight was a mystery like no other.

'It can't be easy for you when you don't know anyone here, Eva.'

'But everyone I've met has been so friendly.'

'So I've noticed.' He glanced around as if to convince himself that the youth had gone. 'Handkerchief?' he suggested.

She had been trying surreptitiously to lick her lips while he was distracted. 'Thank you…'

'I apologise for leaving you to your own devices for so long.'

'You don't need to apologise. I was extremely well looked after.'

He didn't like that any more than she liked Roman monitoring her behaviour at the party. But under the circumstances wasn't it better to call a truce? 'It's a very good party. Thank you for inviting me.'

'I didn't have much option.'

'And neither did I,' she fired back, lifting her chin to confront him.

Who knew what Roman was thinking? There was calculation and even a little humour in his gaze, as if he knew something she didn't. Time to go, she reasoned, but then he broke the standoff between them with a laugh, and the night breeze chose that same moment to ruffle his thick black hair. As he raked it roughly into place she was mesmerised.

'The party isn't over yet, Eva. I take it you didn't find a room for the night?'

She silently thanked the shadows for hiding her burning cheeks. She hadn't even thought to ask.

'That's all right,' Roman soothed as if he had known all along she would forget. 'You'll stay with me. I haven't changed my mind.'

But she had. It would be crazy to stay with him. She had so many fantasies rampaging through her head, but if he touched her. If he—

'Don't look so worried, Eva. All I'm offering is a bed for the night.'

Her eyes narrowed. 'What else would you be offering?'

Her voice might be dismissive, but she was disappointed. She was even a little humiliated to think Roman didn't want to try to get her into his bed.

Perhaps he knew.

No. He couldn't know that bold, brash Eva Skavanga was painfully inexperienced. How shaming would that be? He'd probably laugh. She'd probably join him. It was ridiculous for a woman who carried on as she did to be so naive.

'Problem, Eva?'

'Why do you ask?' she flashed defensively.

'You're frowning again?'

'I don't have a problem.'

Even Eva Skavanga had to remember her manners.

'And I'm very grateful to you for allowing me to stay the night.'

There was no problem. The palazzo was as big as a hotel. Her fantasies would be the closest she'd ever get to Roman. And that was quite close enough.

They had made their way back to the dance floor again. She barely had a chance to register this before one of the girls she'd been talking to earlier pushed her playfully into Roman's arms. Before she could disentangle herself Roman tightened his grip. She stiffened immediately.

'You're not going to cause a scene, I hope, Eva?'

She didn't trust herself to speak while her body was busily registering every tiny shift and change in Roman's muscular frame. 'Surely, I don't have to dance with you?' Her throat tightened on every syllable.

'Would that be so terrible?'

Roman's voice was warm and sexy, and everyone was watching them to see what she would do.

'I don't think you have a choice.'

Didn't she know it! She turned to smile at the other girl, who was now dancing happily with her partner. 'One dance,' she gritted out ungraciously.

'One dance will be more than enough for me,' Roman assured her with amusement.

CHAPTER SEVEN

'NO TRICKS, NO JOKES at my expense, no underhand tactics of any kind,' Eva warned as they stood facing each other on the dance floor. Her body, predictably enough, was going crazy during this speech.

'If only you didn't need me quite so much,' Roman taunted softly. 'If only you could vent your anger openly as you are used to doing, and tell me exactly where you'd like me to go. You'd feel so much better, wouldn't you, Eva?'

Smug bastard. Why had she taken so much trouble tracking him down?

Every nerve ending in her body answered that question.

And she had always prided herself on being strong? Her body was softening, while her nipples were tight little buds of hard rebellion. And as for the rest of her—

It was better not to think about the rest of her. Her frustrated body was responding to Roman as if it had identified a solution to its problem in the shape of a man who knew everything about a woman's needs and how to serve them. And her body was in no rush to let him go. She should have stayed in Skavanga and intensified her campaign against him.

Really? Are you sure that's what you would have preferred to do, rather than come here to this sultry island and dance with this man?

'Round about now,' Roman murmured with his mouth very close to her ear, 'I'm betting you're thinking, why did I take so much trouble tracking him down?'

'What?' The word exploded out of her. Forcing a deep, calming breath into her lungs, she steadied herself before assuring him, 'I'm here, and I'm staying until I get what I want from you.'

Roman laughed. 'You might get more than you expect.'

'I'll just have to take my chances.'

'Indeed you will,' he agreed, testing her bravado by tightening his grip.

'I said, no funny business,' she reminded him as her senses tripped off into hyperspace.

'You wish. Are you comfortable, Eva? Is there enough space between us?'

'Just be glad I'm not wearing stilettos.' She shot a sweet smile at him for the benefit of any onlookers. There could never be enough space between them.

'Should we be moving?' she suggested as the band started to play.

'My apologies,' Roman murmured. 'I was thinking of something else.'

'How flattering.'

'I was just wondering what you're frightened of—'

'I'm not frightened,' she cut in.

'You're very tense…'

Her cheeks were burning. Her body was in turmoil. She could not have anticipated how it would feel to be drawn up close against Roman's hard frame. And she wasn't about to tell him that. 'Dancing with me must be such a chore for you,' she said instead.

'A workload beyond imagining.' Shifting position, he made sure that even more of her was welded to him.

They did move well together…very well.

'People are staring at us. What must they think?'

'That you're new in the village. They're wondering who you are and why you came here with me.'

'I hope they don't think we're in some sort of relationship?'

'Almost certainly.'

'And you don't care?' She gazed up and shook her head.

'I never explain my private life and I certainly don't excuse it.'

She would hold herself stiffly from now on. She wouldn't look at him.

But there was something about Roman that drew her gaze. The quirk of his brow, the curve of his mouth, and that wicked glint in his eyes.

'Do you get some sort of kick out of tormenting me?' she demanded when he surprised her by glancing down with amusement as if he knew her fascination.

'I get a kick out of you staring at me.'

His frankness was alarming.

'And as for teasing you? Yes. I like that too. Let's call it payback, shall we, Eva? Though you must agree there's a type of chemistry between us that's bound to cause comment—'

'I do not agree,' she flashed.

Roman smiled down at her. 'You're so attractive when you're angry. And you'll regret it if you pull away,' he added when the music stopped. 'This next dance is one you shouldn't miss.'

He was smiling that dangerous smile again, and that made her suspicious. 'What's so special about it?'

'Tell me afterwards, Eva.'

'Do you mind if I get my head out of your chest first?'

'Be my guest.'

Wrenching herself back, she noticed people watching them. What did they expect? What were they waiting for?

There was only one certainty: Roman had won another round and there wasn't a damn thing she could do about it.

He loved the way Eva blushed. Dancing with Eva was fun and sexy. He couldn't remember having such a good time. She had natural rhythm, and he enjoyed teasing her. Eva was easy to tease and easy to rouse to passion. Her feelings were near the surface and yet strangely bottled in. When she forgot to be tense, he felt her potential to be wild and free and deeply sensual. Who wouldn't be excited by that? But why did such an attractive woman sell herself so short? Was she really so inexperienced? Eva's reputation did her no favours, he suspected.

She scowled at him as they waited for the next dance to begin. He'd always found dancing the perfect prelude to sex, though he was comfortable with the thought that sex wasn't a compulsory activity. It just surprised him that a woman with Eva's passion was so fiercely attached to chastity. 'You will tell me why eventually,' he murmured.

'I will tell you what?' she snapped defensively.

The elderly matchmakers had picked up his interest in Eva, and he had no intention of disappointing them when the next dance began, though Eva was growing increasingly edgy, as if she suspected she was being set up.

'I don't enjoy dancing,' she said, confirming his thinking by glancing towards the onlookers as if she would like to be one of them. 'I avoid it when I can.'

'In the same way that you avoid men?'

She was shocked into silence for a moment. 'How do you work that out?'

'I hope you're not going to deny it, Eva?'

'I'm just not interested—though I don't expect you to understand. I just don't consider serial dating compulsory—'

'Calm down, Eva. I'm not looking for a fight. It's a free world. You do what you want.'

'I'm relieved to hear it.'

'Sarcasm doesn't suit you. And neither does lying about your interest in men.'

And when she looked ready to go off like a rocket, he explained, 'You tell me one thing while your body tells me something else.'

'I've been dancing,' she snapped, her eyes blazing fire. 'And that requires my body to move, in case you hadn't noticed.'

He laughed. 'Not quite so enthusiastically against mine—though please forgive me if I've misinterpreted the signals.'

She huffed as the music began.

'Has someone hurt you, Eva?'

'I haven't come to the party to discuss my personal

life with you. I'm here for one reason, and one reason only, and that's Skavanga.'

'So you were just born awkward?'

As Roman stared at her with open amusement, Eva's ever-dodgy control valve blew. 'If you mean, do I know how to speak up for myself? Then, yes. I do. And if you mean, do I know how to avoid becoming another statistic for some overconfident bed jockey to brag about? Then, yes. I'm happy to tell you that I can do that too—'

The air rushed out of her as Roman yanked her into his arms.

'Eva,' he growled. 'You talk too much.'

A cheer distracted her. Turning, Eva saw that the bride and groom had just come onto the floor to join them in the traditional dance. Everyone was cheering. Even she forgot Roman's insufferable arrogance and smiled. That was the thing about weddings. You could let yourself go without people thinking you were slightly mad. And this did seem to be what everyone had been waiting for.

The dance had barely begun before the groom swept the bride into his arms and carried her away. That was the other thing about weddings. Sex. It was on everyone's mind, not just the bride and groom.

'What's happening now?' Eva was startled to see the circle reforming around them. 'Must we do this?' She shot an anxious glance at Roman. 'Surely, you've had enough of dancing by now?'

'Eva Skavanga losing her nerve?' he taunted.

'Is it that obvious?' she scoffed.

'Don't worry, Eva. You don't have to do anything. Just leave everything to me.'

'Oh, now I'm reassured.'

Her sarcasm was lost in his arms as the music stopped and Roman kissed her.

It wasn't a polite kiss. It wasn't polite at all. He kissed her firmly and thoroughly, and with a great deal of skill.

She was still reeling from shock when people started cheering. Lights exploded behind her eyes, but no one cared, no one noticed, and then Roman let her go, leaving her trembling in front of him. She covered her mouth as if to hide her arousal. That was her first proper kiss by a man who knew what he was doing. Roman had invaded her mouth with the same confidence he did everything else. And she liked it. She had liked it a lot. Her fantasies were nothing but empty shells compared to that. Roman's lips had been firm and persuasive, and he smelled so good.

The next couple had entered the centre of the ring, and something made her want to watch them. When the time came for them to embrace, the man leaned forward and pecked his partner chastely on each cheek.

'That's it?' She flashed an accusing stare at Roman, who cocked a brow and said nothing.

Of course he said nothing. Count Roman Quisvada was a shameless manipulator. The dance was just a harmless party game, not the prelude to an orgy.

'Problem, Eva?'

'Yes. You.' She stared angrily at him. 'How dare you?'

'How dare I?' Roman enquired lazily, easing onto one hip.

'Don't play the innocent with me,' she flashed. 'I know what you did.'

'I should hope so. But now it's time for us to go—'

'Time for you to go,' she said pointedly.

Ignoring this, he made her a mock bow. 'May I thank you for this dance?'

'If you want a scene?'

'Not especially.' He steadied her as she stumbled in her rush to get away from him. 'Ready to go, Eva?'

With a huff, she stalked off, heading for the shadows at the side of the bar where she could lick her wounds in private. She was still reeling from the kiss. Her body would never forget the sensation. She would never forget how much she longed for more. The suggestive way Roman's tongue had tangled with hers, the touch of his strong warm hands on her naked arms, and the incredible sensation when his body had tightened against her—

And worst of all, her pathetically needy response.

He'd played her like a damn violin in front of everyone.

It wasn't even a proper kiss. It was designed to mock her—to pay her back for her behaviour towards Roman at her sister's wedding, and later at the mine. It was nothing more than a power play.

Well, hooray for him. He'd won another game. But she wasn't nearly finished yet.

'Another dance?' a husky voice behind her suggested dryly. 'Or have I exhausted you, Eva?'

'You've exhausted my patience,' she said, spinning round.

'And if I were the last man on earth…' Leaning back against the bar, Roman smiled down at her, 'You'd still want to go to bed with me. Wouldn't you, Eva?'

'You are—'

'I know what I am,' he cut across her roughly. 'The question is, do you know who you are?'

'You're not even ashamed?'

He shrugged. 'Why should I be? I enjoyed it and so did you.'

'You think?' she derided.

He enjoyed it?

'I know,' he argued, holding her angry stare.

This could have been so much easier to deal with if Roman hadn't been so hot.

And had danger not proved quite so addictive.

'If there are any more gaps in your education, Eva, I'd be only too pleased to fill them in.'

'I bet you would.'

Her mind dropped below his belt. A pulse throbbed insistently between her legs. Her breath caught. Her heart thundered. She should run a mile. But did she want to? Roman's eyes were delivering a challenge straight into hers, and there was a look in his eyes she'd never seen before. Incredible though it seemed, Roman Quisvada wanted to go to bed with her.

He wanted to have sex with her. And he wanted it now.

CHAPTER EIGHT

MAYBE SHE COULD have handled this encounter with Roman better if her experience hadn't been confined to terrorising the local youths in Skavanga.

Maybe not, Eva amended as Roman led her away from the party. Couples were wandering past them arm in arm, their feet in the surf, their gazes fixed on each other, unaware of the silent drama being played out only yards away. A little farther on, Roman nudged her and put his finger over his lips as he drew her past shadowy forms resting on a grassy bank, forms that undulated like waves and sighed like the surf, so Eva couldn't be sure if the sounds she could hear were those of heated passion, or just the sea sliding rhythmically over rock and sand.

The couple didn't even notice them pass. She envied them their ability to lose themselves in each other. Would she ever know what that felt like? That seemed unlikely, since what came naturally to them was an insurmountable obstacle for her.

Roman sensed immediately that something was troubling her. 'Problem, Eva?'

'No,' she lied, glad it was too dark for him to see how

embarrassed she was. Eva Skavanga, embarrassed by a couple making love?

And terrified at the thought of penetrative sex with a man.

How humiliating would that be if Roman knew? And how would those fears play out when they reached the palazzo?

'Watch the loose rocks here,' Roman said, putting a firm hand under her arm. His grip was firm and strong, and, in spite of her turbulent thoughts, she trusted him. She glanced up, wishing she could confide in him, but she could never do that, not where such personal matters were concerned. In Skavanga she took control. She forged the path, but here she was glad of Roman's guiding hand on her arm.

'It's flat now,' he said, letting her go. 'There's nothing you can trip over.'

Except her heart.

'Thanks…'

They walked side by side, but there was too much space between them. She felt the lack of him. She felt the lack of his touch.

'Stay close, Eva.'

She smiled in the darkness. 'I will,' she promised. 'I will dog your footsteps until we have that talk.'

He laughed. 'Is that a promise?'

'You can count on it.'

Roman's laugh was warm, and she tucked it away in her heart. It belonged to tonight, but that didn't mean she couldn't keep it close.

They carried on up the snaking path that led to the palazzo. The grand edifice glittered above them beneath a moonbeam spotlight like an icing-sugar mirage. Eva hoped her own goals were more substantial. She hadn't forgotten why she was on the island, and was as determined as she ever had been to make Roman listen to her concerns.

He'd slowed down for her as the climb was growing steeper and took the chance to ask her if she'd enjoyed the party when she stopped to catch her breath.

'How could I not? Other than when you sold me down the river with that kiss. But I'll get you back.'

'I'm counting on it.'

She sucked in a fast breath, and he guessed she hoped he hadn't heard her. He'd enjoyed the party too. 'Maybe you should get out of Skavanga and test yourself some more.'

'Maybe I should,' she agreed. 'The music was great,' she admitted, leaning back against the rock face. 'It made me happy and sad within the space of a tune. Does that sound crazy?'

His lips pressed down as he shrugged. No more crazy than lingering with this complex girl on the way to taking her to bed. And how could he not be pleased that she shared one of his favourite passions? 'Music touches me too,' he admitted, coming to stand beside her.

Dio! Where was he going with this?

Deeper than he usually went with a woman, that was for sure.

'You make me so angry,' she admitted wryly as she stared into the night.

'I do? You don't seem very angry.'

'Not now.' She smiled as the night breeze lifted her hair. 'But earlier…'

'Ah.' She was referring to that kiss.

She smiled as she stared out across the sea. 'You

make me laugh at myself, Roman, and I guess that's long overdue.'

'You don't expect me to comment, do you?'

'You'd better not,' she warned. And then she turned to him. 'Why do you always tease me?'

'Authority, influence and opportunity.'

She shook her head. 'You are incredible.'

'I like to think so.'

He brushed the hair off her face. They stared at each other for a moment. 'Come on,' he said.

She took his hand. He liked that.

She felt safe with him and that *was* crazy. He made her wish she could be different—bold in every area of her life. He made her wish she could lighten up and have fun—fun that didn't involve scoring the bullseye at darts or playing the winning shot at pool.

Glancing up, she thought the faint tug of his lips was all the reminder needed that a woman as inexperienced as she was really shouldn't be flirting with a man like Roman Quisvada. She let go of his hand. She'd forge her own passage. Eva Skavanga was all about front and fantasy, while Roman was more reality than most women could handle. If he knew the truth about her—the whole truth—he'd probably laugh at her. She'd probably join him. What would he think about her being 'one of the boys' because she'd never had the courage to be 'one of the girls'—to be tested, to be lined up against all the pretty, smart, sassy girls, and fall so far short she wasn't even in the game.

'Am I going too fast for you, Eva?'

Probably. 'No.' She laughed as she forced herself to keep up. This was all going crazy fast.

Roman waited for her at a turn on the path and smiled at her when she drew close. In her fantasies he always took centre stage. How could he not when Roman Quisvada was a natural-born hero? And after that kiss at the wedding…

But in real life? Sexually speaking, he was way too much for her. Better to start with a quiet man, a timid man—

A man you could direct? her cynical inner voice demanded. *Where would that get you?*

Catching hold of her as she went to walk past him, Roman brought her in front of him. 'Are you really so woefully lacking in self-belief, Eva?'

'What? No. What brought that on?'

'I can read you, Eva. I can read you like a book.'

She turned her face away, acutely conscious of Roman's light grip on her naked arms. Lack of self-belief was the least of her problems. The night had closed around them and there was no one in sight… No sounds except for the soft susurration of the surf. Would he kiss her? Would he kiss her again because he wanted to and not to mock her?

Roman answered the question by dipping his head to stare into her eyes. He made her wait. He made her wait until she swayed towards him. She held her breath as he teased her mouth, inviting her to kiss him back. She was longing to enter his dark and very sensual world, where there was no compulsion to join him, but there was an open invitation. Was it possible to be intoxicated by the senses? She thought it might be as Roman kissed her in a way that left no room for reasoned thought. He was rampantly male and unapologetically sexual. He towered over her, and yet there was no suggestion he would use his hugely superior strength to overwhelm her.

Perversely, this made her fantasies run riot, along the lines of being pinned down and subjected to every type of pleasure known to man—and a few she didn't know about that she felt sure he would. Holding her around the waist, Roman used one hand to cup her face, so gently her will ebbed like the tide. Leave it much longer and she would be lost. He made her want more... so much more.

Until his hand slipped down to cup her buttocks. What was natural and instinctive for him was frightening for her. It was too intimate. It was everything she craved, yet feared, and, having lost her confidence, she pulled back.

'Eva?' Roman's lips brushed her mouth, fogging her brain.

A woman of her age afraid of sex?

'Why are you frightened of me?'

'I'm not—okay, maybe I've heard things—' Desperate lie, and she hated herself for it.

'Do you believe everything you hear, Eva?'

He looked at her slender shoulders, pale and vulnerable in the moonlight. He felt strangely protective towards a woman who had done nothing but fight him. He wanted her, but only if Eva came to him because she wanted to, and without the doubts that seemed to dog her. Eva wasn't just another notch on his bedpost. She already connected with some deep part of him that no one else had ever reached. He wanted to bring her pleasure. He wanted to hold her in his arms and—

'Stop!' he yelled as she wandered towards the edge of the cliff. He knew this path like the back of his hand.

She didn't. He didn't need a grudging shaft of moonlight to tell him that was she far too close to the edge. Catching hold of her, he drew her back. His voice gentled. 'Are you going to swim from here? Seriously, don't wander off. Not here. It's too dangerous.'

They had left the party lights a long way behind. There was just the sea in front of them spread out like a glittering cloth touching a star-frosted sky. And one step away from Eva's feet was a yawning void leading to a boulder-strewn beach.

'I…' She turned her face up to him and swallowed awkwardly. She'd clearly had quite a shock. He wanted to kiss her but this time held back.

'What do you say to someone who just saved your life?' she asked him.

'I think we should take it slowly from here?'

Pressing her lips together, she sighed with exasperation, and then said, 'Agreed.'

'Don't sound so worried, Eva. I'll keep you safe—so long as you don't wander off again.'

They stood in silence for quite a while. They had both said more than they had intended to, she guessed, and then Roman's idea of safe was to lead her on towards the palazzo. She had always thought herself in charge of her own fate, but tonight that wasn't going so well.

'I do have to thank you for saving me.'

'However annoying you are, I'm not going to let you fall over a cliff, Eva.'

There was a smile in his voice. She was relieved to hear it. She enjoyed the light banter with Roman, and wanted to tell him that she did trust him, but that she didn't trust herself not to make a mess of things. Stepping off a cliff was the least of it.

'Just one more request,' he said.

She glanced up.

'Can you stop sighing like that? I can't tell if those sighs mean you're excited, reluctant or just plain exhausted.'

'All that dancing and kissing?' she mocked lightly. 'I think I can handle it.'

She knew where this was leading; she'd always known. She could have pulled back at any time. But had she? When they reached the palazzo she'd tell him the truth. It really was that simple. She'd tell Roman frankly that she wasn't going to have sex with him, and that for all her talk she just wasn't that type of girl.

So what type of girl was she?

'Where are you now, Eva?'

'Right by your side.' But she knew what he meant, and Roman was a big man who no doubt had an appetite to match. Her stomach tumbled at the thought of what she'd done. He'd taken her at face value—the kiss *and* her response to it. Eva Skavanga was notoriously passionate, so why wouldn't she be passionate in every area of her life? Perhaps it would be better to tell him now—

'Eva—'

Her heart lurched as Roman turned to face her. She took a step back and found her spine pressed up hard against the smooth rock face with Roman's fists planted either side of her, boxing her in. There was no escape. His stare was keen and all the more compelling lit by moonlight.

'How about you tell me the truth before we get any further into this?'

'How did you—?'

'How did I know? Are you serious? Like I've said before, Eva, I can read you. It isn't that hard. And now I want to know the truth from you—all of it.'

'The truth?' Was this really going to be the moment when she explained that she wasn't the girl everyone thought she was?

Relaxing his arms, Roman stepped back with a shrug. 'Coming here to the island to see me has everything to do with Skavanga, and nothing to do with our meeting at the wedding?'

'Nothing at all,' she said, turning away. 'Can I go now?' She sidestepped him with a smile.

'Be my guest…'

They were only yards from the gates of Roman's palazzo and the gulf between them had never seemed wider. She'd done it again. She'd messed everything up. She didn't know what she wanted, or what she didn't want.

Roman stood back at the gate to let her in. He was so sure of himself, so relaxed. He made no attempt to move aside, which forced her to brush against him. His machismo scorched her. Every nerve in her body fired at once. Her physical self cried out for pleasure, while the old Eva shrank back, already tasting failure.

'Comc on…' Putting his arm around her shoulder, Roman led her forward. He opened the door and took her inside, across the hall and up the stairs, and along the elegant landing. He backed her into his room, his dark stare holding hers. He leaned past her to shut the door.

Her heart went crazy. 'I can't do this.'

'Can't do what, Eva?'

'Whatever it is you expect of me, I can't do it.'

'You're sure of that?'

'I'm certain.'

'How do you know what I want you to do?' The shadow of a smile hovered around his lips. 'I promise not to tell anyone that Eva Skavanga lost her nerve, if you promise not to tell anyone I had to trick you into kissing me.'

'You mean…'

'Do I want to kiss you? What do you think, Eva?'

Dipping his head, Roman kissed her slowly and thoroughly as he backed her towards the bed, and, in spite of all her promises to get herself out of this, her grip on him tightened with every step.

CHAPTER NINE

'IS THIS WHAT you want?' Roman whispered, transferring his kisses to her neck. 'And this?' He teased her ear lobe as she trembled uncontrollably in his arms.

She couldn't speak. Her legs were shaking beneath her. Roman was holding her up while she floated in sensation, and when his big hand found her breast and his skilful fingers got to work, the fact that he could be so delicate, so intuitive, and that he could instil such confidence in her, brought the last of her barriers crashing down.

A sigh shivered out of her as his hand found a warm home between her legs. The shock of Roman touching her intimately was so extreme her mind blanked and she acted instinctively, pressing against his hand in the hunt for more sensation.

Kicking off her sandals, she stumbled in her haste, but Roman was there to steady her, and when her hands were shaking he helped her with her belt and top too.

Everything that had seemed so wrong, so fearful, so utterly beyond her reach, suddenly seemed the most natural thing in the world. She stood watching as Roman undid his belt and left it hanging as he tugged his shirt over his head.

She was in awe of his body. Muscled and hard and tanned, he was magnificent. She wondered then about the simple gold chain he wore around his neck. Roman was such an understated man. Even his wristwatch was plain steel without any of the dials and gizmos she'd noticed other men appeared to need. And the chain was delicate, while Roman Quisvada was most definitely not.

His muscles flexed in the moonlight, which shimmered around him as if even the light was drawn to such a magnificent form.

Her heart leapt when he snapped his belt free from its loops and tossed it aside. Kicking off his shoes, he slid his chinos down deeply tanned, hard-muscled thighs. Naked now apart from a pair of black silk boxers, with his thick black hair in wild disarray, he looked more the barbarian than ever. He was so much taller than she was—so much bigger in every way. She liked the sense of feeling small and protected, and being wanted by a warrior such as this. The width of his shoulders, the washboard stomach, the narrow waist, the legs that seemed banded by steel—he was more than impressive, though she quickly looked away from other contours, lovingly defined beneath the finest silk.

'You're beautiful, Eva.' Reaching out, he touched her hair with such tenderness.

She held her breath as tension sizzled round them. She hadn't stood in front of many men wearing a see-through bra and a thong, if any, and drank in Roman's frank approval. But could she match up to his expectations? She glanced at the bed, wondering about all the impossibly glamorous and sophisticated women he must have known. She drew in a shaking breath. This was crazy. But what would life be without a little crazy in it?

Roman's lazy gaze had a touch of warmth and humour, and it was that that relaxed her. It also made her shiver uncontrollably with lust. She wanted to be close to him. She wanted him to touch her and to draw her into his arms. She wanted to nestle there, rest there… belong there.

Maybe he sensed this, or maybe he wanted it too. She huffed a laugh inwardly. As if. And then asked herself impatiently, why could Eva Skavanga be so bold in every area of her life except this?

Taking hold of her hand, he drew her towards him. What he did next surprised her. He guided her sensitive thumb pad across the kiss-swollen swell of her bottom lip.

'Do you feel that, Eva?'

She felt it in her core.

The corner of Roman's mouth had kicked up as if he felt her responses as if they were his own.

'And what about this?' he prompted.

He took her hand on another sensual journey, and the intensity of sensation made her gasp as he moved the flat of her palm slowly across her nipples. And all the time he held her stare firmly in his, so he could watch her reaction, while her own arousal was heightened by the approval in his eyes. At one time this would have seemed so wicked and wrong, but with Roman, no. He was making her do this to help her accept that she could feel and that she could respond without fear. The sensation was indescribably good, and had a direct link to other places, prompting her to squeeze her thighs together, which produced a pulse of pleasure that drew a shaking moan from her throat.

Roman smiled when he heard this. 'I think you like that,' he said.

Like could not describe that feeling. She only knew she wanted more.

Sensing this, he took her hand on another journey, this time over the sweep of her belly and down the smooth, warm length of her thighs.

'I think you like that too,' he whispered, smiling against her mouth.

'You know I do,' she breathed.

And while she was growing bolder on this journey of exploration, Roman was stroking her buttocks, cupping and moulding them and caressing them in a way that made her arch her back and ask for more. There was no fear this time. He was introducing her to possibility, and the promise of a lot more to come. His easy, relaxed manner reassured her that there was no hurry, no test at the end of this, but just an endless capacity for pleasure within her.

'What do you want most, Eva?'

She exhaled shakily at the sound of Roman's voice and had to bring herself back to a reality that had expanded beyond her wildest imaginings. 'I hardly know what I want,' she admitted honestly. 'I don't even know what I can have.'

'Try to tell me,' Roman coaxed. 'Search your deepest fantasies and tell me what you'd like me to do.'

'Can't you?'

'No,' he whispered, bringing her into the circle of his arms. They were standing by the bed. Roman was holding her with his chin resting lightly on her head.

'You can't keep passing the buck and avoiding the issue. You have to spell it out, Eva.'

'You like to hear it?' she guessed.

'Maybe,' he admitted.

'You're merciless, while I'm a shivering wreck?'

'Shivering with desire,' Roman murmured, nuzzling her neck.

'You know me so well.'

'I can read you, remember?'

'Touch me,' she whispered.

'I am touching you, Eva.'

Yes, and her bones were melting, but it wasn't enough. Roman knew that, just as she knew there was more—if she could only bring herself to ask. But for once in her headstrong, outspoken life, she couldn't find the words.

'Why don't you show me, if you find that easier?' Roman suggested.

'Ramp up the pressure?'

'Why not?' he murmured.

He was testing her. But she could do this. She certainly wanted it enough. Finding his hand, she guided him, only to be rewarded by the most fleeting and frustrating brush of his fingertips.

'That isn't fair.'

'Who says so?' Leaning back, he stared down at her, his voice husky and amused.

'Then I'll take you on a journey.'

'Please.' His stare was dark and not a bit concerned.

She gasped noisily when he cupped her.

'*Dio*, Eva. Do you know how hot you are, how ready, how responsive? Let me pleasure you—'

'Standing up?'

'Why not?'

It seemed so wicked, that was why not. And would her legs even hold her?

'Make it easy for me, Eva…'

Roman's urgent whisper told her what to do. She put her feet wider, easing her legs apart. She felt shy suddenly. Eva Skavanga, shy. In the short time she'd been on Roman's island, he had reduced her to a trembling body of need with only one thought in mind, which was relief from the frustration he had provoked.

This was incredible. Resting her head against the firm wall of his chest, she parted her lips to drag in air. And still he was stroking her everywhere except that one place she needed him. 'You will kill me—'

'I very much doubt that, Eva.'

A shuddering breath gushed noisily out of her as Roman explored her sensitive flesh with his long, lean fingers, always denying her that final contact she so desperately craved.

'You're too eager, Eva. You're in too much of a hurry to reach the end.' Dipping his head, Roman stared into her eyes. 'And I'm going to teach you the benefit of restraint.'

'I don't want to—'

His laugh cut her off. 'Do you have any idea of how ready you are? How hot? How moist? How swollen? But if you want anything more from me, you'll have to tell me exactly what that is.'

'Everything…I want it all.'

'Specifics?' he pressed, showing her no mercy.

Her answer was to shift position in the hope that Roman might not move his hand and she could trick him into touching her.

He laughed softly. 'Naughty.' He had easily anticipated what she was going to do. 'My rules, Eva.'

'So touch me again,' she insisted, turning from penitent and accepting into the old Eva.

Angling his chin, Roman murmured, 'What a relief.'

'What do you mean?'

'I mean, rumours that the firebrand Eva Skavanga has vanished have proved to be wildly exaggerated.'

'You're glad to say?' she queried wryly.

'I'm very happy to say,' Roman confirmed.

'Then get on with it.'

Breath shot out of her as he touched her. The ache was unsustainable. It was beating in her head, behind her eyes and in her ears, drowning out her heartbeat. It was drowning out everything. But this still wasn't enough—

'Touch me, Roman. You know what I need. Don't torture me any longer.'

He laughed soft and deep as he stared down at her. 'You know I love nothing more than to see you burning up with lust.'

'I'll burn if you do as I ask. I'll go out like a damp squib if you don't. You started this and now you must finish it.'

'Finish you, don't you mean?' His firm lips curved in the dark, taunting smile that could always send shock waves of lust racing through her.

'Lie on the bed Eva.'

Her throat closed. Her heart stopped. She was clumsy with desire. Roman had to steady her and help her onto the bed.

'Don't stop this time,' she warned on a shaking breath.

'I'll do everything I can to help you, Eva.'

'Like an interesting project?'

'Like a woman I want to please—the only woman I want to please. Like a woman I want to see come apart with pleasure in my arms.'

'So you enjoy administering and observing pleasure?' she said, making herself comfortable on the bank of cushions.

'I'm going to enjoy administering and observing your pleasure.'

How far had she come? How far had Roman brought her? This was deliciously bad, very bad indeed, but she *wanted* him to watch.

Grabbing the sheet with her inside it, Roman tightened it around her and brought her against his chest. His kiss was hard and urgent. His intention was all too clear. Cupping the back of her head, imprisoning her in a way that made her warm all over, he caressed her cheek with his other hand and stared deep into her eyes as he predicted with amusement, 'It's going to be a long night, Eva.'

It could never be long enough for her. But could she please him without going the whole way? Could she soothe her own frustration? Time was running out. Roman eased onto the bed beside her. She had to decide now, either to speak or to remain silent. She chose silence. Every part of her might be tingling with fear, but her excitement overrode that, and all it took to forget her fear was the thought of what he might do next.

'Come to me, Eva.'

Roman's gaze was steady and commanding. She reached for him and he drew her into his arms. He made her feel so safe. This felt so right. And perhaps because Roman was so relaxed and unhurried, she was able to relax too. He stroked and kissed her anxieties away and she was more than ready when he moved down the bed. First he suckled her nipples, one and then the other, until she was panting with excitement and pleasure, and when his hand slipped between her thighs while he was still doing this she wondered if it was possible to pass out with pleasure.

'Do you want something more, Eva?'

'You know I do.'

'Then you must tell me what it is you want.'

But that seemed so bad. 'No…' Her voice was shaking with frustration.

'Yes.' Roman's voice was pitiless.

'How can I tell you when I don't know?'

'I'll never hurt you. Take it from there, Eva.'

How could she think when her heart was firing like a machine gun? This was all completely natural to Roman, but for her—

She drew a sharp breath in when he slipped a pillow beneath her hips.

'Knees clenched like nutcrackers? Not a great start,' he murmured wryly, smiling up at her. 'Relax, and then tell me how you feel.'

She turned her face away. 'Shy,' she blurted. Determined, she tried again. 'Self-conscious…' Her lips pressed down as she thought about it. 'Excited. And extremely frustrated,' she admitted on an awkward laugh. 'And exposed—but I don't want you to stop.'

Roman laughed. 'So you trust me at last?'

'It would appear so.' The old fire was back in her voice, but there was a smile in her eyes now.

'*Brava*, Eva Skavanga,' Roman's warm breath caressed her ear. 'So is this what you had in mind?'

'Oh, yes…'

'And this?'

One skilful fingertip traced a line of fire exactly where she needed him— Well, not quite. It was always close, but not quite touching…

'You're very responsive, Eva.'

'But I shouldn't—'

'You shouldn't what?' he said as she turned her head away. 'You shouldn't allow yourself to feel pleasure? You shouldn't lose control?'

While she was hesitating over her answer, he removed her tiny thong.

'You don't really need this,' he explained with a smile when she gave a shaking cry. 'And I wouldn't worry about losing control if I were you. That's going to be something you'll have to get used to.'

'If you say so.'

'I do say so. My rules, remember?'

'I love your rules—in this context only,' she quickly said. She loved the way he cradled her as he fondled her, parting her lips and working with one finger, so delicately and skilfully, in a way that almost instantly brought her to the edge.

'Good,' he murmured as she sucked in a great shuddering breath.

She moaned with pleasure, needing this so badly, and so unutterably grateful that Roman knew everything there was to know about pleasure and how to please her.

'Look at me, Eva. Yes. Look at me.'

'If I promise to look at you, will you touch me again?'

'Are you making bargains with me?' He smiled into her eyes.

'Would you prefer me not to? Would you prefer me

to accept everything and be meek and mild, or would you rather I was true to myself, Roman?'

'I wouldn't know you if you were meek and mild,' he admitted. 'But I do have just one question to ask.'

'Which is?'

'Whose rules do you think will bring you more pleasure, Eva? Yours? Or mine?'

Her rules? *Pleasure me, endlessly. How? I'm not sure. I'm no good at this—*

Or his rules? *Pleasure me endlessly. You know exactly how—*

'Your rules. At least for now,' she tempered.

CHAPTER TEN

'RULE NUMBER ONE: you do exactly as I say. Rule number two: you don't lose control until I tell you that you can.'

Rules? Seriously? Her mind was shooting splinters into the ether just at the prospect of release. If those were his rules she would sign up now.

'Only when I tell you,' Roman repeated as if he knew the innermost workings of her mind. 'It might not be as easy as you think.'

'I'll risk it.' He knew she was on the edge. He knew she wouldn't need much pushing.

'Don't even think it. Take your mind somewhere else.'

'But how am I supposed to—?'

'To stop yourself?' Roman supplied. 'You'll do that easily when you remember that I won't touch you again if you don't.'

She nodded tensely.

'Do as I say and the pleasure will continue as much as you want for as long as you want. Disobey me, and it will stop immediately.'

'I'll obey you in this one thing,' she made clear.

'And gladly, I would have thought,' Roman murmured, a sexy smile playing round his lips. 'As for the rest?' His stare grew frighteningly dark and compelling. 'It's all up for grabs.'

Hmm. Roman was a maestro and she was the orchestra he had chosen to direct. The ache inside her had reached crisis point. She was in no mood to argue. 'I agree to your conditions.'

'We're both adults. Everyone's at the wedding, so you can be as noisy and as uninhibited as you like.'

She nodded agreement as if she understood, but she was wondering if Roman was always so calculating—there was no other word for it. Was he incapable of feeling? She had imagined her first real sexual experience would be very different from this. She had hazily imagined some romantic encounter with an ordinary man, rather than a high-achieving sexual athlete. Was this what she wanted?

As she thought about it Roman was holding her in a loose embrace, and her hand somehow strayed to the fine gold chain he wore around his neck. She pulled back to take a better look at it. He removed her hand. *Don't touch.* She got it. But why?

Did she have to know everything about Roman? What did she want out of this? Wasn't the fact that he was experienced enough for her? So he had nothing more to give other than pleasure? That wasn't so bad, was it? Was she such an expert in returning normal human affection? They both had boundaries they refused to cross—

'Are you still a virgin?'

'What?' She was startled by the question hitting her out of the blue.

'Maybe not a virgin,' Roman said thoughtfully. 'But as close as it gets…'

She laughed as if she knew all about it. 'How can you be close to being a virgin? You either are or you're not, surely?'

'You should have told me,' Roman said, drawing back.

'Told you what?' she asked defensively, but she knew. 'I can just imagine that conversation.'

Roman frowned. 'What's so difficult about telling the truth?'

She couldn't answer him, and after a long moment he shrugged and brought her back into his arms. She didn't wait this time. She didn't want any more questions or explanations, she just wanted him to touch her, and when he did her screams of release could probably be heard in the village.

'Good?' he murmured when she had quietened a little.

'What do you think?'

'I think more,' he said.

'If I must,' she whispered, glancing up at him. Her hips were already working against his hand.

'Once is never enough,' Roman agreed, moving down the bed.

'What are you doing?' She barely got the question out before she reacted fast and violently to the touch of his tongue and his lips and his hands and his—

'And again?' he suggested.

'Definitely.' She was still panting for breath, but instead of feeling sated she was gasping for more.

Her eyes shot wide as Roman slipped one finger inside her. 'Does that hurt?' he whispered.

She needed a moment before she could speak—a moment to get used to the sensation…the invasion, the shock. And during that moment Roman began to stimulate her with his other hand, so in seconds she had forgotten why she had been frightened.

'Good?'

Like she never wanted it to end good. 'Yes…'

'And now?' he said, slipping another finger inside her.

'Yes… Oh, yes.'

While Eva gained in confidence and grew used to the new sensation, he kept her arousal high. He was in no hurry. They had all night. She soon forgot her fears and rose against him, seeking more, and as she did so his free hand slipped round her back to support her and he felt the scar. It wasn't small, and it wasn't deep, but it was a ragged expanse of damaged skin that didn't strike him as the result of falling out of a tree as a child, or even a more serious accident that would have required treatment in hospital. It was perhaps a burn, or a severe grazing episode that had been coped with at home. He wondered about it, but said nothing. This wasn't the time, not for either of them, but it gave him another piece of the jigsaw that was Eva Skavanga.

Perhaps the scar answered everything. Eva was a beautiful woman who was neither completely innocent nor experienced. She had kept the world at bay, maybe because she had been hurt badly at some time. Whatever else he had discovered about her tonight, she brought out his protective instincts.

Was this the start of a relationship?

Forget that. He would have to learn to care long-term—to risk his heart, his pride, his slumbering emotions—and he just wasn't cut out for that.

'What are you doing?' Eva exclaimed when he reached into a bedside drawer.

'Protecting you,' he said, ripping the foil. 'Would you like to—'

Her face turned grey.

'Would I like to what?' she whispered.

'Would you like to put it on for me?' he offered, pressing the packet into her hand.

'I don't think so.'

Her confidence died a little more as he threw back the sheet.

He waited. And waited. Finally she huffed a laugh, but it sounded brittle to him. She didn't want to take things any further. He didn't need it spelling out. He doubted she had taken things this far in the past. His concern for Eva took a huge leap. If a man took her at face value Eva could find herself in serious trouble at some point down the line. 'Don't know how to?' he suggested.

'Don't be so ridiculous,' she flashed, pulling the sheet tight around her. 'You really are one arrogant piece of work, aren't you?'

'*I* am?' Sitting up, he reached forward and took her hands in his, forcing her to look at him. 'You're playing a very dangerous game, Eva.'

'How so?' she demanded.

'You're lying naked in a bed with me.'

'I didn't notice you fighting me off.'

'When I have sex with someone, I have to be sure.' As he spoke he was swinging off the bed and standing up. 'Call me old-fashioned, but sex is a mutual pact, as far as I'm concerned, requiring absolute trust between two people.'

'Are you sure you wouldn't like to draw up a contract first?' she suggested, pulling the sheet tighter still.

'It is a contract. It might be unspoken and unwritten, but it's a contract all the same.'

'So sex is just another form of business for you—a cold-blooded operation. Have I got that right?'

He shook his head. 'You know I don't think that.'

'So it's an enjoyable pastime that you indulge in with women who know the score?'

His lips pressed down as he considered this. 'Women who are looking for the same thing from me I am from them,' he agreed.

'Meaningless sex, you mean?'

'Mutual pleasure,' he argued mildly. 'Don't go on fooling yourself, Eva. Don't live a lie—'

'Is that your homily for the day over and done with?' she interrupted.

'Don't be sarcastic, either. It doesn't suit you. And you know I'm right.'

'Do I?' she said, grimacing.

'You can't live your life based on a lie.' As he should know. 'At some point you have to come clean and admit who you really are to yourself. So you're not experienced? Do you imagine I think any less of you for that? Regular sex isn't some sort of pre-qualification in the game of life. Some people remain virgins for ever, and are quite happy to do so. You can't force these things, Eva. If it happens it happens. If it doesn't—'

'You'd know all about that, I suppose?' She'd grown tense.

'Look—why don't you just lock your door tonight if that makes you feel better?' he said, moving away.

'And what about your mixed signals?' There were tears in her eyes now. She couldn't understand what had happened. Neither could he. He had wanted this as much as Eva—more, probably.

'You kissed me,' she said in a small voice that tore at his heart.

'I did,' he agreed.

'Was it so terrible?'

He couldn't stand this any more and dragged her into his arms. 'It wasn't terrible at all.'

'I've never met anyone like you,' she said angrily, pulling away. 'First you tell me I'm coming on too strong, and then you do exactly that. How do you expect me to take that in my stride?'

'I don't expect you to,' he said frankly, raking his hair with frustration. 'The trouble, Eva, is that you're not just a good actress—brilliant sometimes—you're as hot as hell.'

She shook her head as if trying to understand what he was saying. 'You think you know me, but we've only known each other five minutes.'

'How long should it take?' he said quietly.

'Oh, I forgot. You're more perceptive than any other man.'

'Maybe.' He shrugged. 'Where you're concerned.'

'And what's that supposed to mean?'

She sniffed loudly, wiping her nose on the back of

her hand in a way that touched him more than any seductive look she might have given him could hope to do. 'It means I'm going to bed, Eva. And so are you. But in your bedroom, not mine.'

CHAPTER ELEVEN

'WHERE ARE YOU GOING?' she exclaimed as Roman walked towards the door.

Eva wasn't a nuisance, or even a girl he wanted to take to bed. She was a lost soul searching for meaning in a complex world, and unfortunately she had chosen the wrong person to help her to do that. 'I'm going to take a shower. I suggest you do the same. There's another bathroom across the hall. There's a robe hanging on the back of the door you can use. Get to bed, Eva. We have an early start in the morning.'

'Going where?'

'Going somewhere I hope will help you to understand what I do, and why you don't need to be worried about the mine. You can find your bedroom from here?'

'Of course.'

'Then goodnight, Eva…'

She wasn't reassured, and flung the pillows aside as she sprang off the bed.

Eva's spirited departure was somewhat marred by getting tangled up in the sheets, forcing him to return to free her.

'Don't touch me,' she warned. 'And as for us having an early start in the morning? I wouldn't count on that if I were you.'

'Oh?' he queried mildly. 'I thought you were eager to discuss Skavanga with me? Or doesn't that matter so much now?'

Her eyes widened at this, and then her lips firmed. He guessed she was longing to say something with a sting in its tail, but managed to stop herself in time. 'I am eager to discuss Skavanga,' she confirmed. 'What time shall we meet?'

He hid his pleasure that she was as big a person as he thought she was, and his voice gave nothing away. 'Six a.m. in the hall. Don't be late. I have a flight plan filed. Wear jeans.'

'You don't need to see me out,' she told him as he followed her to the door.

'Forgive my good manners. I'm on my way to open the door for you—and to close it behind you. I don't want to risk you slamming it in my face.' He opened the door and held it wide. 'I'll see you in the morning, Eva.'

'Not if I see you first,' she muttered.

She was incredibly stung that Roman could be so businesslike after what had happened between them. She wanted to be pleased that their passionate encounter had ended without cause for regret, but all the old insecurities had kicked in, and now she was back in her own room she couldn't shake the feeling that she'd been sampled and discarded. This was not the fantasy she had scripted, featuring the dark count, who, after listening to her impassioned pleading, would turn out to have a marshmallow heart. This was just a mess.

They had been briefly close and now she felt they

were further away than ever. So why had she pulled back? Why couldn't she go through with something she had always dreamed about? What was wrong with her? Why was it easy being strong in Skavanga, but here everything fell apart? What about those goals she had set herself before she came here? And what about building something instead of destroying everything she touched? And why…weirdly why, she was asking herself, would it have been different if Roman hadn't been such a gentleman? In her fantasies it was all about being pinned down and pleasured to death, while in reality it was more complex, especially when the hero turned out to be just that: a hero.

She was falling in love with him, Eva realised, hugging herself as she leaned her head against the bathroom door. There would be no one after Roman Quisvada. How could there be? But love was out of the question; he'd always made that clear. Roman had never once allowed her to think that there was anything in his heart for anyone. He approached sex like food and ate when he was hungry. She knew the deal.

Closing her eyes, she allowed herself a few self-indulgent seconds of self-pity before reminding herself that she had come here for a purpose, and that her goal was still in sight. Hadn't Roman said they were going somewhere tomorrow that would fill in the gaps for her, and that it had everything to do with the mine? She should thank him for bringing this farce to an end. He had forced her to refocus on the only thing that mattered, and that was Skavanga.

So why did she feel so empty?

Because now she knew that Roman was so much

more than she had imagined. She had fallen in love with a fantasy hero, but Roman Quisvada was all too real.

She ran a bath and still he was in her head—and it had nothing to do with his incredible body, or the force field of sex that swirled around him. Or even the humour in his eyes. It was the man. Stripped of his wealth and his obvious attractions, Roman was special, while she was too shy, too awkward, too inexperienced, to have a hope of holding his attention. He made her see things differently. He made her want to rush home and hug her sisters, and tell them they must never fall out again—that *she* must never fall out with them again. He made her see that sometimes it was better to hold back and think things through before rushing off in her usual headstrong way. But she wasn't the only one with secrets. Roman had his share. She wanted to know him better. She wanted to know his secrets…

She thought about Roman for so long the water grew chilly. Was there a chance he would come to her tonight?

There was always a chance…

There were no sounds in the big house when she padded barefoot into the bedroom. It was so romantic with moonlight streaming into the room and across the covers on the bed. And it was all wasted on her. Awkward Eva had done it again. Drawing the toweling robe a little closer, she firmed her jaw. Tomorrow was another day. And Roman had promised they would talk. Look at it that way, and it was mission accomplished.

But then she would go home and nothing would change, and the idea of becoming an increasingly embittered old shrew held scant appeal.

It didn't have to be this way.

Padding over to the main door, she opened it a crack, and then a little bit more. It wasn't exactly an invitation. It could even be taken for a door left open by mistake. But if Roman should happen to notice, and came in…

Was that likely?

Throwing back the covers, she climbed in between the cool sheets and stretched out. Closing her eyes, she steadied her breathing. She lay tensely listening for what felt like hours. Once she even heard a door open, but it was somewhere far away and soon closed again. After that, silence mocked her, and, defeated, she fell back on the pillows. Roman had no intention of visiting her tonight—or any other night—and she was a fool to think he might.

She tossed and turned throughout the endless night, searching for sleep and finding very little, so that by the time she woke it was with surprise that she had slept at all. There wasn't even time for breakfast—just a quick shower. She made it down into the hall at the same moment that Roman powered through the door.

'Ready?' he said, already turning to go.

It took her a moment to reply. She was still reeling from the slam into her senses of seeing him again. 'Where *are* we going?'

'To open your mind, Signorina Skavanga.'

'That sounds interesting.' And if she didn't rush he'd be gone.

They were together again. She couldn't help a little inward jig, because right now that was enough.

Striding at speed down the path that led through the gardens, Roman took her through a rose arbour, which was a miracle in itself in such a hot climate, and then on across to a perfectly manicured lawn where sprinklers were on active duty. The tall, arching spray glittered a frame around the outline of a sleek white helicopter. The helicopter was empty. So Roman must be the pilot. Of course he was.

'Duck your head,' he warned as they approached the long blades. Opening the door, he gestured for her to get in. Once she was settled, he passed her a set of headphones. 'Put these on. I'll help you strap in.'

She braced herself for the moment when his hands brushed her body. It was important that she behaved as if nothing had happened between them—as if he hadn't seen her naked—as if he hadn't taken her to the door of paradise and slammed it in her face.

'Problem, Eva?' he said, standing back.

Slamming doors was a theme between them? She bit her lip to hide her smile. Everything was happening so fast. 'I didn't expect this.'

'The ferry's too slow for what I've got in mind,' Roman said as he checked her straps.

He smelled amazing and looked even better. She doubted he ever took the ferry. She doubted she could survive being with him in such an enclosed space.

He closed her door, which gave her a few brief seconds of isolation in which to collect her thoughts. No chance. There could never be enough time for that while Roman was around. Evcn the air seemed to jangle when he climbed in beside her. It was charged with his energy, as was she. Just watching him strap in and put his headphones on, before placing a brief call in Italian to some distant control tower, was arousing. His familiarity with the big machine as he flipped switches and made other preparations for take-off was ridiculously sexy. His naked arms, tanned and coated with just the right amount of black hair, were sexy. His strong hands and wrists brought back memories of an extremely sexual nature, while his crisp short-sleeved shirt, tucked into well-packed jeans cinched with a no-nonsense leather belt, only made her remember what his body felt like beneath his clothes. And it tempted her gaze to wander down—

'Are you sitting comfortably, Eva?'

His voice with its metallic twang as it came through the headphones startled her. Raising her chin just in time, she said, 'Fine, thank you.' Mighty fine.

Roman turned back to his pre-flight checks. His harsh, unyielding profile, with the customary coating of stubble, was incredibly sexy. Roman Quisvada was the most compelling individual she'd ever met, and she had to force herself not to take in any more of him and just stare straight ahead.

Before she knew it the ground was sinking away through the worryingly see-through panel on the floor at her feet. As she watched, the island became a playroom carpet of bright colours: green, orange, brown and blue.

'Can you hear me clearly?' Roman checked, bringing her back with relief to the reassuring sight of him in full control of the situation.

'Perfectly, thank you.'

'And you're not nervous?'

Tongue in cheek: in what context? 'Not one bit,' she confirmed.

'Good. We'll be in the air around an hour.'

'Are you going to tell me where we're going now?'

'To one of my facilities on the mainland. And you don't need to shout. I can hear *you* perfectly too.'

'I thought your work was cutting and polishing diamonds?'

'It is.'

'So that's where we're going?'

Roman didn't answer. He had started talking to someone on the other end of the radio link, and so she fell silent, frustrated by the lack of information. Roman always contrived to be one step ahead of her, and that was something she had to change.

Heat rushed through her as, conversation over, Roman turned to glance at her. 'I'm going to teach you all I know, Eva.'

About diamonds? There was a suspicious amount of humour, even in the robotic tone of voice coming through her headphones. So long as it wasn't her klutzy lack of skill when it came to Roman's advanced class last night.

'Diamonds can do more than buy a woman or ruin a man.'

'That's a very jaundiced view.'

'Perhaps I have a very jaundiced view of life, Eva.'

Perhaps he did.

Her thoughts turned from daydreams to reality as the glittering blue ocean gave way to pristine white seashore and then on to neatly cultivated land where the soil was a rich shade of ochre. It was some time more before she spotted any real signs of habitation other than the occasional farmhouse or barn, but then came increasingly busy roads and small towns, until they were hovering over what looked like a brand new industrial park.

'Welcome to Quisvada Industries, Eva,' Roman announced as he took them down. He landed the helicopter exactly on the centre of a yellow cross in the middle of a number of immaculately maintained, pristine white buildings. 'This is where we cut and polish the diamonds.' He switched off the engines and signalled that she could remove her headphones now. 'And where we do a few more things you probably won't be expecting.'

Diamonds, always diamonds. Her mind rioted with impatience. Would she never escape them? Why were diamonds so important to everyone but her? Yes, she wanted the mine to survive, but she couldn't help wishing that Skavanga could be saved by some other means. Couldn't Roman see she was desperate to get their talks under way? She was grateful to him for taking this time out to show her round, but she was desperate to move on so they could talk and she could go home. There was only so much torture she could take and she was just about at her limit. Being close to him, yet poles apart in their thinking, was unendurable. 'I know all about diamonds,' she exclaimed with frustration, ripping the headphones from her head.

'No,' Roman argued as he dipped his sunglasses down his nose. 'You only think you do.'

He was right again. Their visit to his facility was a revelation for her. Everyone had heard about industrial diamonds, though Eva hadn't realised that the demand for them far outstripped gem-quality diamonds.

'Although the use of synthetic diamonds is on the march,' Roman explained.

And he was on top of that too, Eva realised as he took her through another sterile white building. 'I must admit I wasn't aware of the many uses of industrial diamonds in medical situations.' She paused and spoke her next words with care, sensing Roman's particular interest in this subject as his hand strayed to the gold chain he wore. 'I knew that diamond dust was used to coat various medical instruments, but I had no idea that it was used to target rogue cells.'

'The list goes on and on,' he confirmed.

She had wondered about Roman's obvious obsession with the medical application of diamond dust, as explained to Eva by one of the technicians working in that particular department. Roman's eyes had gleamed with fervour as he had stood beside her listening.

'Our boss is one of the biggest supporters of medical research in the world,' the technician had told her proudly. 'Without him there would be no progress.'

'It might be slower, Marco,' Roman tempered, resting his hand on the man's shoulder, 'though I appreciate your confidence in me. But I can tell you, Eva, that without people like Marco nothing would be achieved.'

More surprises were in store when Roman took her for lunch. He chose a low-key beach shack rather than some high-tone restaurant.

And this was better, she thought as they kicked off their shoes. She could relax and be herself—maybe even forget who she was for a couple of hours, forget who Roman was and their respective roles in life. She could forget the fact that she was having lunch with a billionaire who just happened to have flown her here in his helicopter.

'Is that okay for you?' Roman checked with her when the handsome young waiter suggested the fresh catch of the day for lunch.

'Perfect,' she confirmed, resting back in the wicker chair. 'This is heaven.' And after the ups and downs of the past couple of days, to be sitting like this with her feet in the sand and Roman at her side, with the lazy surf rolling rhythmically back and forth in between them, this was heaven.

'Have I convinced you?' he asked in a lazy drawl, leaning back.

She smiled as his chair creaked. It hardly seemed substantial enough to contain such a significant force. 'I can see the need for those diamonds now, and it goes far beyond what I thought…'

'But?' he queried, sensing a question in her words.

She waited until the waiter had served their cold drinks. 'I suppose your particular interest in the medical application fascinates me. You seem…' She hesitated.

'Unusually passionate?' Roman suggested. 'That's because I am.'

'It wasn't your passion that surprised me. It's the direction it takes. Is there some particular reason for that?' she asked carefully. 'A personal reason, perhaps?'

He shrugged and finished his glass of water, pouring another before he spoke, and then he just said, 'Yes.'

She waited, but then their food arrived and they were both distracted for a few moments. When everything had calmed down, she tried again. 'So…'

'Eat, Eva. Your food will get cold, and it looks delicious.'

'Yes, it does,' she agreed, but she didn't make any move to pick up her knife and fork.

'All right,' Roman threatened as he shook out her napkin and spread it across her knees. 'I'll have to feed you if you won't eat. You have been warned.'

'No. Seriously. Please tell me—' She jumped in with both feet. 'Starting with the gold chain…I can tell it means a lot to you. Why do you wear it?'

When his eyes flashed she was sure she had gone too far too soon, and wished she could call the words back, but Roman quickly gathered himself.

'It was my mother's chain. She got sick and died,' he said briskly, unemotionally. 'I'm just trying to do some good, Eva. We all have to do what we can, even if it's all too late. So now you know. Do you mind if we eat now?'

'I'm sorry. I didn't mean to pry. It's just that I don't know too much about you apart from what I read in the newspapers.'

'And that's largely lies and exaggeration.'

She shrugged and smiled briefly as their glances met and held for an instant. 'I wouldn't know, would I?'

A long moment passed, and then Roman said, 'My adoptive mother died—my blood mother too…of the same illness.'

'Fate can be very cruel sometimes,' she said gently, treasuring his confidence in telling her what he had.

'I still can't believe it all these years on.'

Roman seemed lost to her for a moment. 'It was a terrible coincidence,' she said quietly, not wanting to intrude on his painful memories.

'I still blame myself,' Roman revealed as he stared out across a deceptively placid-looking ocean.

'You can't blame yourself for their illness.'

'I blame myself for causing them the stress that might have provoked it,' Roman explained. 'I grew up the trophy son, praised to high heaven by my adoptive parents, but when I found out the truth about my birth on my fourteenth birthday, all I wanted was to be accepted by my blood family, but when I went to find them, they shut the door in my face.'

'It was too late and your mother had died?' she guessed.

Roman's smile lacked any humour. 'Worse. It was the day of her funeral, and having her fourteen-year-old son turn up out of the blue was the last thing her grieving family had expected. She bore more children after me, and it was just too much for them, my turning up, and at the worst time possible. They told me to my face I had no place there.'

'So you believed you didn't belong anywhere.'

'My adoptive parents took me back without question and with open arms.'

'But that was good, surely?'

Darkness still lurked behind his eyes. 'They had never shown me anything but love—and how did I repay them? By becoming increasingly cold and unfeeling.'

'But you were so young. You must have been so full of anger and bewilderment.'

'And now it's too late.'

'It's never too late,' she whispered.

'All I wanted was to make them proud.'

'And don't you think you have?'

'I should have loved them more at the time, and then thought about making them proud of me. My adoptive mother fell ill, but I didn't even notice I was so self-obsessed.'

'Most teenagers are,' Eva pointed out. So this was what had put that haunted look in his eyes. Her heart ached for him. 'You've never forgiven yourself, and yet you must have been broken-hearted too. What a terrible shock for you, and teenage boys don't deal too well with emotional upheaval—'

'Which of course you know all about,' he snapped,

resenting her intrusion into his hidden world, she guessed.

'I do know, as it happens. I have a brother, Tyr, remember? I only have to think back to remember Tyr rampaging around the house, yelling at everyone when he was young because he had no other outlet for his feelings.'

'So that's how you learned to shout,' Roman said, slowly coming out of his black mood.

In that moment, things changed between them. An understanding grew that hadn't been there before. 'My personality has nothing to do with my brother, Tyr—though, like most sisters, I blame him for lots of things, but not that.'

'So you just grew this way?' Roman suggested, a smile curving his lips.

'I don't know what you mean,' she said, acting menacing.

'I think you do know, Eva.'

This was too much—too much emotion—too much understanding of what made her tick. She chose not to meet Roman's penetrating stare, and stared out to sea instead, to where the heat-bleached horizon met the intense blue-green of deep water.

Perhaps if Tyr had stayed home rather than answering the wanderlust that had always plagued him, things might have turned out differently, but like Roman she couldn't turn the clock back. She didn't want to. Things were as they were, and she was as she was, and for once in her life, sitting here next to Roman, that didn't seem such a very bad thing.

CHAPTER TWELVE

STANDING UP, HE held out his hand to Eva. She hesitated. Then she smiled and reached out to him. He drew her with him, pausing only at the counter to pay.

'We'll be back.' Roman narrowed his eyes when it struck him that the gaze of the smiling waiter taking his money was fixed longingly on Eva's face.

His hackles rose. He smoothed them down again. Who could blame the youth when Eva looked as she did—a little bewildered and surprised she could enjoy herself and relax as she had with him? She was endearingly dishevelled from the stiff breeze blowing off the sea, and her face was flushed from the warm sun on her winter pale skin. She looked beautiful. She looked beautiful and vulnerable and desirable, yet strong. She was as strong as he was, maybe. But she was tender too, and sensitive. He had never told anyone the history of the chain he wore, or his backstory. Only the two men in the consortium knew that, and they had known him since school. And though they had hardly known each other long, he trusted her, and for no better reason that he knew his diamonds, and Eva was a pure blue-white in a grimy world. She was everything he had dreamed about as a teenager, and as a man could never find.

'Where are you taking me now?' she asked him as they headed back towards the helicopter.

'That depends on whether you're prepared to call a truce or not,' he teased her, drawing her along by the hand, wondering if he had ever felt quite so relaxed or so happy with a woman. 'Personally, I think you owe me for showing you around.' His face relaxed in a smile as he stared down at her.

She met his gaze and smiled. 'I'm not sure I'm quite in the same league as you, Roman. I don't have a helicopter to whisk you away, or a multimillion-pound facility to blow your mind.'

'How about a return trip to Skavanga?'

'Are you serious?' The smile died and was replaced by something far more touching.

'Never more so,' he said.

'Then it's a date,' she said, brightening at once.

There weren't many women who could persuade him to change his plans. Eva could, because he wanted to please her. But he still wasn't sure he could break the habit of a lifetime and learn to feel again, so for Eva's sake he had decided on a delaying tactic he thought she might enjoy before they made the trip to Skavanga. 'We're going somewhere else first.'

'Where?' she asked him when they reached the helicopter.

'Get in and I'll tell you.'

'Roman?' she prompted while he was buckling her in.

'Close.' His lips curved in a smile as he settled the headphones on her head. 'We're going to Rome.'

She looked at him. 'Why not Rome?' He shrugged, stood back and closed her door.

'Explain,' she demanded through the headphones the instant they were in the air.

'I have an apartment in Rome.'

'Of course you do.' She sighed with resignation.

'It's a city apartment and I think you'll like it.'

'But all my clothes are at the palazzo.'

One rucksack and a heavy parka? 'So we'll buy some more.'

'Life is always so simple for you.' She didn't sound pleased. 'And no. *We* will not buy some more clothes for me. What do you think I am?'

'A small shareholder in the mining company I've invested in. Just call it an advance on your next dividend.'

That silenced her—for around ten seconds. 'That sounds very confident.'

'I'm a very confident man, Signorina Skavanga.'

'I noticed,' she murmured beneath her breath.

This was amazing, Eva thought as Roman led her through the grand entrance into a tiled courtyard of what had to be one of the most magnificent buildings in Rome. To describe this as a city apartment hardly did it justice. If there was one thing she had noticed about billionaires—bearing in mind she only knew one—it was that they were masters of understatement. And they certainly knew how to rack up the miles. Distance meant nothing to them. Hotels were redundant. Roman appeared to have a home in every worthwhile stopping off point in the world.

And Rome was definitely worthwhile, Eva reflected, marvelling at the grandiose surroundings as the cool of plaster walls and marble floors soothed her heated senses. Roman had pointed out all the unbelievably well preserved historical sites as they were driven from the airport to the city. To see ancient buildings co-existing next to very modern structures was astonishing. The modern city of Rome had been built around artefacts that left history intact as a lasting reminder that everyone carried a legacy from the past. The Coliseum was so much bigger than she had imagined, and infinitely more menacing, while the Vatican City with its stunning rococo architecture was breath-taking. Roman had asked their driver to stop at the Trevi Fountain, where he had pointed out the statue of Oceanus, god of all the waters, who gazed out sternly from his horse-drawn shell chariot, which was guarded by conch shell blowing tritons.

'It's magnificent…'

'You'll have to come back here one day,' Roman had teased her when they got out of the car to take a closer look. She had stood gaping like the country bumpkin she was. And then he had pressed a coin into her hand, and when she had asked him what it was for he'd told her to toss it over her shoulder into the water, and she would come back… She'd laughed, but she did as he said. Hearing the coin splash into the water had made her think about all the other wishes it was joining. Had any of them come true? she had wondered.

'Eva?'

'Sorry.' She shook herself round, realising Roman was waiting for her to cross the shady courtyard and join him.

'The security is for the Italian president, not me,' he murmured discreetly when she gazed at the security guards in their dark suits and dark glasses. 'We share the same building,' he explained.

'Of course you do,' she said wryly. 'No. Seriously,' she added, teasing him with what was fast becoming their catchphrase, 'I believe you.' They both laughed.

'Would you like to go out for supper tonight?' Roman asked as he ushered her in through an ancient ornate door.

She clocked the butler in his dark, beautifully tailored dark suit, who had appeared seemingly out of nowhere to open the door for them, and who now faded into the background, as if he worked on astral orders rather than spoken instruction.

'Eva?'

'Sorry.' She shook her head in an attempt to shake herself round from all the surprises. 'I was distracted.'

'I was just saying—or would you prefer to stay in?'

'Oh, go out,' she said quickly, and then blushed, realising how naive she must sound to him, but she longed to see something of the city while she was here. And also, after her last disaster in the bedroom, staying in seemed by far the riskier choice.

'Let's say, we'll meet in an hour,' Roman said with easy charm, glancing at his watch. 'If you need me you can reach me on the internal phone. My number's one.'

'No. Seriously?'

She got the killer smile for that.

'At least it's easy to remember,' she said, tongue in cheek.

A housekeeper in a dark uniform took over from Roman to show Eva the way to her fabulous suite of rooms. There were high ceilings, gracious furnishings and beautiful mouldings on the pale silk-covered walls. All the many fascinating architectural details had been renovated with respect and skill. The quality of everything was unsurpassed. Even the air seemed to hold a particular scent. Money, she thought, reverently running her fingertips across a gilded console table. On the top of the table was a single turquoise vase. White roses had been arranged in this together with fragrant spikes of lavender. The scent was indescribably lovely. She could scorn such extreme wealth all she liked, but Roman's money would save Skavanga, just as it had allowed him to restore this historic building. Perhaps she needed to rethink her beliefs a little. She was beginning to wonder if some of her less worthy campaigns hadn't been an escape from her insecurities, and a chance to expend some of her frustrated sexual energy.

Having examined every inch of the sitting room overlooking one of Rome's most impressive squares, and then her equally lavish bedroom, bathroom and dressing room, she kicked off her shoes and threw herself down on the vast bed. But there was no time to bask in these fabulous surroundings. She must be ready to go out and explore Rome in less than an hour. Explore Rome with Roman. That was as perfect as it got.

She took a bath in the gloriously restored bathroom, where the best technology and efficient plumbing existed happily side by side with stained-glass windows and marble pillars. She could have basked in warm suds all night, but shot up hearing a knock on the door. It definitely wasn't Roman. His rap was unmistakeable and this was a polite knock.

Wrapped in a robe with her hair in a towel, she opened the door. The landing was deserted, and it was only when she turned back to the room that she saw the gown rail packed with the most amazing clothes. This was flanked by a line of carrier bags from possibly every exclusive store in Rome. Closing the door, she went to investigate and found handbags, underwear, shoes, shawls, and—

'Roman Quisvada, come here this minute,' she blasted down the phone. 'No, I won't take no for an answer. How did you guess I wasn't going to accept your largesse? Don't you know me yet? You're sure I must like something? If you want to take me to supper, you can take me as I come or not at all.'

'Is that a promise?' he drawled.

'You—' She growled at the silent receiver in her hand. Roman was on his way to 'help her pick out an outfit', apparently. That should go well!

A sense of anticipation gripped him as he approached Eva's suite of rooms. It was useless telling himself this was wrong, and that she was a baby and he was not. A fiery baby, maybe, but an innocent one, none the less.

So why was he taking the stairs two at a time?

Because he wanted her and she wanted him. Why complicate things?

He knocked on the door. She swung it wide. 'Problem?' he said, walking in.

'This,' she said, gesturing at the gown rail. 'An advance on my dividend? Do you know how small my personal investment in the mine is? I'll never be able to pay you back for all this.'

'So don't keep all of them. Choose one.'

'Even one of these outfits would take me a decade of dividends to pay off. And what's wrong with what I'm wearing?' she said, indicating her jeans. 'Or are you ashamed to be seen with me?'

'Not at all. I don't even know what makes you think

that. I just thought it would be nice for you to have some clothes to choose from.'

And he was right. It was better than nice. Did she have to throw every gesture back in his face? 'I just feel awkward,' she admitted. 'I'm not used to all this fuss. It was very thoughtful of you, but it's too much.'

'I'm just trying to save time. Stop ranting and start dressing is my advice, or we'll lose our table.'

'I hardly think that's likely.' Bearing in mind who had booked that table, but she was hungry, and—

'Look, Eva. If you're so worried about paying me back, why don't you come and work for me?'

The bombshell dropped out of the blue, and she had nothing to say to that. No speech prepared.

Roman shrugged as he walked deeper into the room. 'Come work for me,' he said as if this were the most obvious solution in the world. 'You don't want to be a freeloader. And I'm not trying to buy you. So pay your way. That's fine by me. My aide Mark pulled your CV and I've read it. Your qualifications are every bit as good as Britt's, so why have you never used them? What's your problem, Eva? What are you frightened of?'

'I'm not frightened of anything,' she scoffed, blushing as she turned away, but curiosity got the better of her in the end. 'What type of job?'

'Well, let's see now,' Roman murmured as he flicked through the dresses on the rail. 'I think this one. What do you think?' He held up an elegant dream of a dress in navy blue silk. 'I think this colour would look wonderful with your hair.'

'You haven't answered my question.'

'I've got some good ideas, and that's all you need to

know right now. Try this on. We can talk about work over supper.'

'You talk and I listen, presumably?'

'We'll both talk and we'll both listen,' Roman countered, holding her gaze. 'I thought working on behalf of the mine was what you wanted, Eva?'

'I'll listen to what you have to say. Of course, I will,' she added, wanting to sound receptive rather than belligerent for once in her life. She didn't dare to hope that tonight her wishes could all come true at once.

Roman had judged the supper perfectly. He had a deft touch when it came to matching setting with mood, and had chosen a warm little womb of a place where it was impossible not to feel relaxed. Bustling and busy, the decor, in shades of red and old gold, was slightly old-fashioned and slightly shabby and all the better for it. The owner greeted Roman in a way that suggested he had been eating in the same place for years, and there was an air of confidence about the restaurant that suggested it had been in the same family for generations. There were quiet booths, soft lighting, and a jazz singer performing wistful songs at low volume at a piano in the corner. Eva and Roman occupied an end booth where they had more privacy than most.

'I couldn't eat another thing,' she assured him when the waiter brought their coffee. The food had been delicious, but it was hard to concentrate on anything other than the fact that they were sitting across a narrow table from each other with their knees almost touching.

'You look lovely, Eva. I'm glad you like the dress.'

Almost without realising it, she smoothed the skirt.

She had never owned anything quite so elegant. She lived her life in jeans or polar trousers, so the dress was quite a departure from her usual style. She was glad he didn't gloat that she'd given in. There were battles worth fighting, she had learned, and others where no one lost by backing off.

'You're frowning again.'

'Thinking about that job you mentioned,' she admitted. 'Are you serious?'

'Never more so. You have qualifications in land management, specialising in polar regions, so why haven't you put them to use?'

'I had family commitments—and I don't want to talk about that now.'

'So I talk and you don't? I don't think so, Eva. That's not how it works.'

'This was your idea, and either you have a job for me or you don't.'

Roman looked at her ruefully. 'You might want to think about how that sounds to a prospective employer. Relax, Eva. This isn't a test. It's a serious offer. Maybe the consortium needs your particular local experience and expertise. Have you considered that?'

Her heart wrenched as she realised she was back into the old combative ways, trying to destroy something before she had given it a chance. Was she going to throw this away too? 'Sorry. I'm just—'

'Confused by being thrown into a whole new world of possibility? I know. I know you need time, but there is no time, Eva. We both know the mine is at a turning point, and I'm determined it's going to survive. Now, either you want to be part of that or you don't.'

'Can you tell me something about the job?'

'I want you to work with me.'

'What? Work with you? Doing what?' She had imagined some office job low down the pecking order—something to keep her off his back, yet under his thumb. 'I don't know anything about polishing diamonds.'

'Fortunately, I hire many experts who do,' Roman explained. 'That isn't the opportunity I'm talking about. I don't just plunder mines, Eva. I repair the land and improve it where I can, and that's where you come in. Sit on our advisory board. You're the best qualified person I know to offer local knowledge.'

She drew her head back in astonishment. 'You really are serious.'

'Absolutely,' Roman confirmed. 'Work with me to restore the land after the drilling has established the main shaft. I'd also like you to think about creating a mining museum, something of interest to all those eco-tourists you're so keen to attract.'

Her heart leapt in all sorts of directions. This was a dream come true, but with a catch. Could she work with him? Could she see Roman every day and not want him? Could she watch him get on with his life—get married eventually, and possibly have children? Could she do all that for the sake of Skavanga?

She had to. She must.

She remained mute and thoughtful as Roman paid the bill and exchanged pleasantries with the owner.

'Time to leave,' Roman murmured, making her jump. 'You can decide on the way.'

'About the job?' she said, frowning. 'You're not giving me much time.'

'What else would I be talking about?' Roman demanded, but there was a wicked glint in his eyes that she could hardly miss, and her wilful body responded as he knew it would, right on cue.

CHAPTER THIRTEEN

THEY WALKED BACK to his apartment from the restaurant. It was one of those warm, velvet nights when it would be a crime to sit in a limousine. He wanted to walk through the city he loved, and he wanted to share the experience with Eva. He wanted to prolong the evening and that was rare for him. What Eva thought about his city mattered to him, and as he watched her she reminded him of when he was a boy, and Rome had amazed him. He hadn't always been as sophisticated as she thought him. He'd grown up wild on a tiny island, but he'd made his first fortune here by wheedling himself into the employ of one of the top jewellers by touting the title he'd never used before. That had been his first taste of a world that thought a lot of titles, whereas he knew from his blood father's example that a title added nothing to the quality of a man. Roman hadn't been too proud to use that title—not if it got him where he wanted to be. He believed it was the least that was owed to him by the man who had sold him to a mafia don.

'I love this city,' Eva breathed as they strolled past the Coliseum. 'There can't be anywhere else like this place on earth.'

Eva was an easy companion and he wasn't used to

that. Most women were in a rush, either to get into his bed or into his wallet, but Eva was different. She was like a plant that had been buried beneath polar ice, and was only now pushing a few tentative green shoots towards the sun. Yes, he wanted her. And no, he wasn't usually this romantic where women were concerned. In the past he had always made it clear that neither love nor romance, let alone marriage, would ever be on his agenda. He'd seen where love took people, and it wasn't pretty. He preferred to make a straightforward pact where each party got what they wanted from the other. And that had always been enough for him.

'Well, we're here,' Eva said, slightly anxiously, he thought as they reached the entrance to his home.

The customary duo of men with earpieces and suspicious bulges beneath their jackets was leaning back against the wall. He nodded to them. They nodded to him. He didn't pause to speak. There was something he couldn't wait to do, and he didn't need an audience for that.

'What are you doing?' Eva gasped as he swung her round and backed her against the door as soon as he had let them both in. 'Where's the butler?' she added nervously, gazing about.

He laughed. 'Only you could worry about the butler at a time like this. If you want a drink, I'll get it for you,' he added huskily.

'I don't want a drink.'

She was a little breathless, a little flushed. She was perfect. 'I think I prefer this new, bashful Eva—'

'As opposed to the old grouch I used to be?' she cut in, giving him one of her wry smiles. 'Just because we've had a nice supper, doesn't give you the right to insult me.'

'But it does give me the right to kiss you.'

'Says who?' she said, frowning a warning at him.

'Says me. And don't worry,' he added dryly. 'You can be as uninhibited as you like. I gave the staff the night off.'

Arrogant, her narrowed eyes told him. 'I've heard something like that before,' she said.

'And as I remember, you weren't too displeased with the outcome.'

'Ah,' she murmured as he brushed her mouth with his.

'Shall we go inside and continue this in greater comfort?' he suggested.

'Yes, why don't we do?'

His senses roared. One moment she was the innocent, and the next Eva was like no other woman he had ever known. There was only one certainty and that was that he wanted her. And this time she wouldn't say no. He deepened the kiss and she softened against him. He closed his arms around her and she pressed her body into his. His erection thrust against her. She moved a little, and then with more confidence, taking her pleasure from him. He cupped the back of her head and laced his fingers in her wild, silky hair. She groaned deep in her throat in response. He lifted her and carried her the rest of the way to his bedroom, and when she saw that his bed faced the lights of the city through the floor-to-ceiling windows, she gasped.

'No history lessons now,' he warned as he lay her carefully down on the bed.

'I hope you're going to join me?' she said.

'I've got nowhere else to go.'

Laughing, she reached out for him. 'Am I ever going to knock that arrogance gene out of your system?'

'I doubt it,' he murmured, starting on her zip.

Kicking her shoes off, she pushed the jacket from his shoulders and unbuttoned his shirt. He shrugged it off, and by the time he'd slung it on a chair and turned around she'd taken off her dress. He moved back to the bed, and she reached for the buckle on his belt. Unfastening it, she freed it from the loops and then reached for the button above his zipper. They did that at the same moment and their fingers tangled. They laughed, and he left her to it. He stood in low-slung boxers staring down at the woman on his bed, wondering how he ever got so lucky.

'Are we overdressed?' she queried, putting a cheeky finger beneath her chin as she stared up at him.

'You definitely are,' he said, viewing her bra and pants.

'And you're not,' she said, hooking her fingers into the waistband of his boxers. 'Do you have something in that nightstand to rectify that situation?'

'Might have.'

He sat on the edge of the bed, toying with her hair. He didn't want to rush a moment of this. Tiny auburn curls framed her face and a fan of gold-red hair cascaded across his snow-white pillows. She looked like a promise and a dream all wrapped in one. And, hell no. He was not a born-again romantic. It was simply a fact.

She wanted him so much and this felt so right that all the fear had left her. Their previous disastrous encounter had faded into oblivion. She had changed and so had he. Roman had deepened. He had revealed more about himself, so she knew now that he was more than a warrior in business, or an irresistible sexual animal—he was a man like any other with all the same struggles and flaws, and that was what made him perfect.

She felt close to Roman in a way she had never felt close to anyone before. But she needed to be closer still. She longed to be one with him. This wasn't a whim, or a need to prove she could overcome her fears or even a memory to lock away of one night with an incredible man. Her feelings went so much deeper than that. It was something she couldn't put a name to, unless she called it love. And yes, she was taking an incredible risk with a man who had always laid his cards on the table. She was risking her heart and her pride and her future happiness, but none of that mattered. Nothing added up to this. Only Roman making love to her was important now. Nothing else came close.

Roman stretched out beside her and took her in his arms. He was leisurely and confident, as if they had been lovers for years. She felt so safe in his arms, and so turned on. Roman's body was magnificent, but it was the man beneath the rugged frame who would keep her safe. This was like no feeling on earth. Every part of her was singing with arousal, and every part of her was primed and ready for whatever would come next…in her heart, in her body, in her soul. She was desperate for physical release, but every time she sighed and clung to him like a desperado, he smiled against her mouth and held her back. 'You can't keep me waiting for ever.'

'But I can try,' he argued.

'This is one battle I won't let you win.' Reaching up, she laced her fingers through his hair. Feeling it spring against her palm, as strong and virile as he was, was the ultimate torture, and then he added to that torment by rasping his stubble across her neck.

'You're merciless,' she gasped as sensation shimmered through her.

'Lucky for you…' Roman smiled wickedly against her mouth.

'You're right,' she agreed, panting. 'I deserve this.'

'For however long it takes?'

'Oh, I hope so.'

'We could be here some time.'

'I'm planning on it.'

Breath left her body in a rush as Roman swung her beneath him. He judged the weight of his body on hers, supporting most of it on his arms as he nuzzled her mouth, her lips, her eyes, her forehead, not forgetting the very sensitive lobes of her ears before moving on to her neck. And then he kissed her mouth, and she floated away on a sea of sensation…wanting more… always wanting more.

She gave a shaking cry as he lodged a thigh between hers.

'Not yet. You have to wait, Eva.'

'Why?' Her voice was shaking with need.

'You know why—'

'Let me,' she said, taking the packet from his hand. 'Lie back.'

'And think of England?' he teased.

'Stockholm, please… Though perhaps you'd do better thinking what a mess I'm going to make of this.' She was only half joking.

'You are not going to make a mess of anything, Eva. You operate complex machinery in Skavanga, don't you? This should be well within your technical capabilities. I'm pretty sure my aide's exhaustive report mentioned your expertise with power tools.'

'Yes to all the above. But unfortunately, I don't have too much experience with machines that can feel or are quite this complex.'

'Damn. And there was me thinking you were going to say you weren't used to dealing with machines of this complexity and size.'

They laughed and she forgot to be worried. Because she trusted him, Eva realised. And because she loved him. What could possibly go wrong?

Nothing went wrong. Roman drew her beneath him and she was soon lost in sensation; he saw to that. When his hand found her she was more than ready and she didn't even flinch when he brushed his erection against her, teasing her with the tip. He finally eased carefully inside her and when she was used to the new sensation, he almost brought her to the brink with shallow strokes. It was a happy shock to find she wanted more. Give and take, thrust and relax, rise and fall, arch and subside, rhythmically, eagerly… She was greedy to take more of him than she would have believed possible. Turned out she had quite a talent, Eva realised as Roman groaned with pleasure as she drew him in.

'I'm supposed to be telling you to wait,' he growled against her ear.

'And now you're having a problem? Think drill bits and diamonds and you'll be fine.'

'You think?'

She wasn't doing too much thinking, as she was right on the edge herself, and could only give in gracefully as Roman pressed her knees back and upped the pace.

'That's so unfair,' she said when speech was possible. 'You didn't even give me a warning.'

'Did you need one?'

'No,' she decided, thinking about it. 'I like to be surprised.'

'Big surprises as often as possible?' Roman guessed.

'All the time.'

'More?'

'What do you think?' She rose against him, welcoming him back.

They made love all night. Neither of them tired. Why would they be? She had waited a long time for this, and Roman was inexhaustible. They were well matched. Turned out she was a closet nymphomaniac, and Roman had the answer to her every need.

'There's one thing I don't understand,' he said as they lay with their limbs entwined during one of their brief resting periods.

'Tell me,' she managed groggily, easing comfortably against him. Roman was so big and she was so small, and yet every part of them fitted so perfectly together. How did that happen?

'Why were you frightened of men?'

She lifted her head, suddenly wide awake. 'I'm not afraid of men.'

'Really?' Roman murmured. 'So why haven't you had any affairs, Eva? You're not exactly a troll.'

'Well, thank you for that,' she mocked. 'And how do you know I haven't had hundreds of affairs?' But then she remembered Roman's people in Skavanga and their famous reports.

'I don't believe you've ever allowed a man to kiss you

as I kiss you, because that would put too much power in their hands.'

'Now you're being ridiculous.'

'Am I?'

There were some things she never talked about, and she was in no mood to spoil the moment.

'Relax, Eva. You don't have to tell me anything you don't want to tell me.'

But the craziest thing of all was that she wanted to tell him everything, but the memories had been buried so long she couldn't just flaunt them as if they meant nothing. She didn't trust herself to go back to that dark place just yet without losing it—without losing him and losing all the gains she had made in confidence.

'You can't blame me for being curious about the woman who slammed the door on me at the wedding,' Roman murmured against the top of her head. 'Eva the firebrand. Eva the so-called undateable sister—according to my source,' he quickly said. 'And, yes, it gets worse,' he warned, tongue in cheek.

'Don't tell me. Eva the shrew? Eva the pain-in-the-butt campaigner.'

'There are quite a few choice epithets for me to choose from,' Roman admitted. 'And some of it I have experienced firsthand, of course.'

'Lucky for you, I can hear your smile.'

'But nothing I've heard fits the woman I just made love to. So who are you really, Eva Skavanga? Are you the beautiful woman who gave herself so completely to me just now? Or are you the frightened little girl sitting at the top of the stairs, listening to her parents arguing?'

'How did you...?' Roman's sources, she realised.

Their *damned* reports. He must have been investigating her from the moment she landed on the island.

'I'm sorry, Eva.' Feeling how tense she was suddenly, he hooked some wild strands of hair behind her ears. She turned away. 'Look at me,' he whispered. 'It didn't take too much working out. And I don't mean to hurt you or pry.'

She relaxed as he drew her back into his arms. 'Then don't,' she said.

'I didn't mean to stir ugly memories.'

But he had. Would she never be allowed to forget? They remained in silence for a long time. She knew Roman wanted her to tell him what had happened, and that he would listen when she did tell him, and without judging her.

'So what about you?' she said, avoiding the question she had successfully avoided for so long. 'Have you never been in love, Roman?'

His sudden stillness gave her an answer, but not the answer she was looking for. He had withdrawn from her and that frightened her. It was like a hint of things to come. And now she was seriously overreacting, Eva thought, until he said, 'I have never made any secret of the fact that love is not what I offer.'

The change in his tone chilled her. After all they'd shared was that all she was –a sexual partner and nothing more? Even friendship between them would be better than that, so much better, though she hated herself for wanting more, because it seemed so weak. 'So you offer spectacular sex and a good deal of spoiling if that's what a woman wants. Expensive gifts and lavish trips to exotic places.' When all she wanted was the chance to love and be loved, and to find a safe haven for her children, should she be lucky enough to have children one day.

'Eva?' he prompted when she fell silent after this outburst.

It had taken a giant leap of faith to trust Roman Quisvada, having grown up associating men with pain and unhappiness. Having seen her father mistreat her mother had left a lasting legacy, and the way she dealt with it was by trying to drive men away. 'I don't want to talk about it.' She turned her head away.

'I'm sorry if I've been hard on you. You don't deserve it, Eva. You're not to blame for my bad handling of the past, or for my colourful history. In fact, you're probably my salvation, Eva Skavanga.'

'You're apologising?' she said, lifting her head. 'You do know I'm the most awkward person I know. It's me who should be apologizing.' She waited. 'You're supposed to be reassuring me now,' she pointed out.

Roman looked at her with amusement. 'We're quite a pair, you and I. You stop me looking back, and I keep you more or less calm. But you should trust me enough by now to tell me what's riding you, Eva.'

'I don't need counselling.' She turned her face away again.

'But you do need to let the poison out. Your sisters don't have a problem, so I have to ask myself, what happened to Eva that didn't happen to them? What did you see that they didn't? What did you experience?'

'Stop it,' she flashed. 'You want to know about the scar. Why don't you come right out and say it? I know you've felt it.'

'I wasn't going to make an issue out of it. It doesn't matter to me, but it obviously matters to you. I'm guessing it must have happened when you were still at home and Britt had left for university and your sister Leila was out of the house—'

'Oh, you're very smart.'

'You have to stop with the compliments. Truly, my head is big enough.'

'You can joke about this?'

'It's better than hiding it away and allowing it to fester all these years. So?' he pressed.

'You're still interrogating me?'

'Yes, I am. And I won't let up. Not now.'

She remained silent for a long time and then it all came pouring out. 'My father began to drink when the mine started failing. He'd come home and beat my mother,' she said without any emotion in her voice. 'You were right in guessing that Britt was away at university, and Leila always seemed to be at some friend or other's after school. He chose his times carefully. I was a bit of a loner and used to stay at school late, reading in the library, but one day I came home early and caught him hitting my mother with his belt. She was on her hands and knees in front of him, cowering. I went for him. I didn't stop to think, I just…went for him. He knocked me away and grabbed the first thing that came to hand. His hat was on the table—harmless enough—but in his fury at being interrupted, at being found out, I suppose, his hand landed on the coffee pot instead. Don't look at me like that. He didn't mean to throw the coffee at me. And I don't want your pity, Roman. I don't want anyone's pity. I came out of it okay.'

'Did you?'

'My mother looked after me. We made a pact that

I wouldn't go to hospital, so long as my father never touched her again.'

'And he kept his word?'

'Yes, he did. That was the end of it. So it was all worth it in the end.'

Roman said nothing.

CHAPTER FOURTEEN

'PLEASE DON'T LOOK at me like that. I've already told you I don't want your pity.' Eva stared at him fiercely. 'And while we're on the subject of secrets and lies, what's so wonderful about your life, Roman? I'm sure you have secrets.'

'My life?' His lips curved in thought as he took himself back to a life that had been built on one set of foundations, only to have those foundations kicked away when he was fourteen. The next twenty years had been spent creating his own set of principles based on anything other than loving, because he'd seen where that led. But now he felt free for the first time in his life—free from guilt, and free from bitterness, because he could see where the future could lead, and that was to a small town in the Arctic Circle and a mining company he would care for as he cared for all his industries. Skavanga Mining had given him a new goal and a new purpose, and, most importantly, it had brought him a girl called Eva.

'The son of a mafia don has certain responsibilities,' he explained. 'When I discovered the truth about my birth I thought I could just shake all those responsibilities off and let my cousin Matteo take over. The island and the village were nothing to do with me any more. I left in a furious rage and that energy helped me to make my first fortune, but the island called me back. The people called me back. I'd never really left them,' he realised as he thought back. 'The bad days of guns and violence were long over by then and Matteo's business had been legitimate for some time. We started working together and I made my second fortune.'

'But the people of the island still think of you as their don.'

'Yes, they do. There are some traditions that can never be eradicated just because you think they should be. And I want to help. I want to do everything I can to help them. And now I realise how lucky I am to have that chance. It's not just a lifelong responsibility as I thought when I was a boy—it's a privilege.'

'You love them,' she suggested.

'I love them,' Roman admitted gruffly. 'And when did you become so perceptive, Signorina Skavanga?'

'Around the time I stopped looking inwards and started looking out?'

'Quite a recent occurrence, then?' Roman suggested, not even bothering to hide his smile.

'Quite recent,' she admitted, reaching for him.

Roman would come to Skavanga to see Eva's concerns for himself and then they would discuss how best to utilise her time in order to progress all the exciting plans she had in mind, both for the mining museum and for the protected ecological park. Her heart was flying on autopilot with no immediate plans to land as she packed her backpack in Rome prior to flying home with him. This was more than she had dreamed of. Working directly for Roman had been the last outcome she had anticipated when she arrived on his island, but then she hadn't planned on falling in love with him either. Snapping the padlock on her backpack, she checked around the lovely rooms in his Roman apartment one last time.

He was speaking on his mobile phone when she came down to the hall. Her footsteps were silent in trainers. He couldn't know she was there. She planned to surprise him with a kiss. She hadn't planned on eavesdropping, but sound travelled in the lofty hall.

'The drilling is completed?' Roman confirmed. 'And the land around the drilling site has been made good? Yes. I'm leaving now and bringing Eva with me. The timing couldn't be better—'

She hunkered down on the marble step, wishing she had stayed a few seconds longer in her room. Her mother used to warn her that you never heard anything good of yourself if you listened in to other people's conversations, but now she had to hear the rest.

'Yes, I'm sure she'll take the job,' Roman continued. 'So, yes, that's another problem solved.' He laughed. 'My line of persuasion is none of your business—though I imagine it's rather similar to your own.'

Who was Roman talking to? His tone was too familiar for him to be speaking to a member of staff.

'Okay, Sharif. Leave it with me…'

He was talking to Britt's husband, Sheikh Sharif, and from the tone of his voice she felt she had been under discussion long before she sat on the stairs. She shivered involuntarily, hugging herself as if a cold, arctic blast had just intruded on her happy and all too blissful ignorance. Roman was ready to leave with his bag at his feet, and a heavy jacket, suitable for polar conditions, slung over his shoulders. While she suddenly didn't want to go anywhere, let alone face the truth.

'Eva,' he said with apparent delight when he spotted her. 'What are you doing like a little girl lost, sitting on the stairs? Come down here and join me...'

As Roman held out his hands, she hesitated. She still had a really bad feeling. By his own admission Roman was incapable of love, and, with all that talk of timing and persuasion, she suspected that his keeping her at his side was just a ruse until it suited him to let her go.

'Come on,' he coaxed. 'What's wrong with you?'

Her world had just caved in. She had grown soft and trusting in his company, and maybe she should have known better. Until she knew the real reason for Roman prolonging her visit, she couldn't bring herself to meekly smile and fold.

'Don't,' she warned as he crossed the hall towards her.

'What do you mean, don't?' Mounting the stairs two at a time, he took hold of her hands and lifted her up in front of him. 'Why won't you look at me? What's happened? What's wrong?'

She shrugged, finding it hard to express a feeling... a suspicion. 'I heard you on the phone,' she admitted finally, avoiding his gaze.

'And what exactly do you think you overheard?'

'That all this delay has all been part of your plan.'

'What delay? And what plan?' he said, frowning.

'Your plan to keep me with you until the drilling is finished and the land is made good.'

'So?' He gave a shrug and shook his head. 'What's so wrong with that? Was I supposed to suspend all the work we're doing at the mine until you returned?'

'You were supposed to be honest with me.'

'I have been honest with you.'

Roman's voice had gained an edge. She should have taken it as a warning that the one thing that fired him beyond all others was to have his honesty questioned. 'You were talking about how you persuaded me to stay.'

'And you heard half a conversation, and on that basis alone you decide not to trust me?' Roman shook his head as if suddenly something was very clear to him. 'I don't think you'll ever trust me, Eva. I don't think that whatever I do, it will ever be enough for you.'

'You seduced me and kept me with you—'

'And I didn't hear you complaining.'

'You kept me out of the way so I couldn't cause any trouble at the mine.'

'Is that what you believe? Surely you're not still so lacking in confidence? I'm coming back with you. Isn't that enough? Doesn't my commitment to you and to the mine mean anything to you?'

'Now the work is done you've got nothing to lose.'

Roman stiffened. 'I can't believe you just said that, Eva.'

'You can't tell me that your motives are completely innocent.'

'I can. And I do,' he insisted. 'And I'm insulted if you think anything different.'

But now she'd started it all had to come out. 'You used me—'

'And you used me,' he fired back. 'Didn't we both have our own agendas at the start of this relationship? Didn't we change those agendas as we got to know each other? I know I did. And, guess what, Eva? We both have flaws. We're not perfect, either of us. And if you can't live with that—' He turned away and made an impatient gesture. 'I wanted you and I thought you wanted me, but now I wonder if I'm wasting my time.'

She heard everything he said and knew every word was true. She also knew her confidence was built on sand and it made her say things before she thought them through. 'Is it time to go?' she asked, wishing she could erase the past few minutes.

Roman was silent for a moment. She worried when he didn't move. And with good cause, she realised, when he said, 'Any time you like, Eva.'

'What do you mean?' Her voice was small. Her shocked words echoed eerily in the lofty hall. 'Aren't you coming with me?'

'You leave Rome now,' he said. 'I'll follow you to Skavanga—' he shrugged as if it might never happen '—at some later date. It's for the best, Eva. If I come with you now, you'll always have that suspicion lurking. You'll always wonder if I kept you with me just to suit my business purpose. Better you go now and get on with this job. I was serious when I said we need your input. And we need it now. This is a job you say you long for, and I want to know how things go—daily reports. Concentrate on that for a while.'

'And then?' She felt chilled to the bone as she waited for his answer. Had nothing changed for either of them? Was Roman still as cold deep down? Was she as defensive as ever? Had she ruined everything again?

'I think you need time to decide what it is you really want, Eva. You can take the jet. It's fuelled and ready. My driver will take you to the steps of the plane and you can fly to Skavanga and start working on the mining projects as soon as you like. And if you want we can pretend this visit never happened.'

That was the last thing she wanted—the very last thing. 'Is that all it means to you?' She spread her arms, lost for words to describe the enormity of the loss she was suffering.

'We're not talking about me, Eva. We're talking about you. I want you to find out what it is you want out of life. I want you to take all the passion out of your thinking and coolly decide.'

'You mean, leave without you?' Her brain was barely functioning. She couldn't throw herself at him and say this had all been some terrible mistake, and could they please get in the car now, because Roman was right, she did need to decide what she wanted. But he did too. She had believed she was on the cusp of something big with him, something special, but if he didn't feel the same way—

'You'll be safe,' he said, mistaking her hesitation for concern. 'You'll be accompanied by my people all the way, and I'll let your sisters know you're coming home so they'll be waiting for you.'

He'd thought of everything. 'Thank you. I'll be fine.' She lifted her chin and even raised a smile. 'You'll have my first report the day after tomorrow, if that suits you?'

'I'd expect nothing less of you.' Roman smiled too, but it was a difficult smile that seemed to hold regret at their parting rather than anything else.

Was that it?

Yes, that was it, Eva realised as Roman punched in some number on his phone and made the arrangements necessary for her solo departure.

* * *

Why was she moping around when there was so much to do? She had landed the job of her dreams, Eva reminded herself firmly as she unpacked her case back home in her bedroom in Skavanga. It would keep her so busy she wouldn't have a moment to miss Roman.

Was she kidding?

She had ruined everything again. Flopping down on the bed, she stared at the ceiling. Planning would distract her from what she'd lost, she reasoned. What she'd never had, Eva conceded ruefully. Roman was not on offer. Never had been, except in her head. And even accepting that didn't help one bit with the ache in her heart.

So leap up. Think about work. Make plans to get stuck into the job—and take things steady this time.

Before she did that there was another very important thing she had to do. She had tried to ring Britt from the airport the moment Roman's jet had landed, but had been told that her sister was in a meeting at the mine. She placed another call now, only to be told the same thing. Recognising Eva's voice, Britt's secretary immediately offered to put her through.

'No, please don't disturb my sister. I'll just dump my bag, then I'll come over there and wait for her.'

'You'll wait for her? Are you sure, Ms Skavanga?'

'Absolutely certain.' God, she must have been such a bitch. She could hardly bear to think about how she must have run people ragged.

On the way to the office she picked out the biggest bunch of flowers she could find on the high street for Britt's secretary, and another one for Britt. She was going to make up for her past behaviour with everything she'd got.

Members of staff could hardly hide their surprise at the sight of Eva Skavanga sitting meekly waiting in Reception, and many came to whisper and stare. No doubt she'd be the subject of gossip for some time to come. It was her own fault, and she'd suffer it gladly, because it wasn't important compared to what she had come here to do.

'Eva?' Britt rushed across the lobby from her office with her arms open wide. She looked as amazing as ever. Businesslike and beautiful. And glowing.

'Marriage suits you,' Eva commented warmly when Britt finally released her.

'Sharif suits me,' Britt admitted softly as she brushed a strand of Eva's wild red hair away from her face. It was a little wilder than usual after the long plane flight as Eva had been so busy fretting about what lay ahead of her—as well as what lay in the recent past—that she had taken advantage of none of the plush private jet's opulent facilities.

'And how about you and Roman?' Britt asked carefully, sensing all was not right.

'There is no me and Roman. And that's not what I've come to talk about,' Eva said over her sister's protest. 'I've come to apologise.'

'To apologise.' Britt pulled a face. 'For what?'

'Now you've made me feel worse than ever.'

'And why's that?' Britt queried, putting her arm around Eva's shoulder to lead her into a quiet office where she could shut the door so they could be alone.

'Because my bad behaviour—my ranting and general carry-on—is so commonplace to you, you probably don't even remember that we fell out just before I left Skavanga for Roman's island. But we did fall out—or at least, I did—and I have regretted it ever since, just as I regret every time I yelled at you for no good reason when you and Leila are the best sisters in the world, and I've not only taken you for granted, but I've abused your good nature—'

'Oh, for goodness' sake, stop,' Britt exclaimed, dragging her close. 'I've never heard anything so soppy in my life. I love you and Leila loves you, and nothing you could ever say or do can change that. But there is just one thing,' Britt added, turning thoughtful.

'Tell me.'

'You can protest all you like that there is no you and Roman, but something prompted this confession. So whatever version of events you're trying to sell me, I'm not buying it.'

'So we're okay?'

'Eva…' Britt shook her head as she threw her sister a wry smile. 'We've never been anything but okay.'

CHAPTER FIFTEEN

ALMOST TWO MONTHS had passed. *Two* interminable months. Confrontation had never frightened Roman. His business life was composed of little else. In business he made objective decisions. With Eva that had never been possible, because always emotion got in the way. He resented every angry word and thought they'd shared. In hindsight they all seemed such a waste of passion. These past couple of months had been the hardest of his life. He had wanted to give her a fair shot at a job she had told him she had always dreamed of. He wanted to give her a chance to cool down from the nuclear fusion that occurred every time they were together. Unfortunately, two months had proved to be in no way long enough for the initials Eva had carved in his heart to heal.

'Sharif—yes?' he said, absent-mindedly picking up the phone.

'Not Sharif. I'm just using his phone, Roman.'

'Britt?' he sat up, instantly anxious. 'Is everything all right? Is Eva okay?'

'Is everything okay with us? Yes,' she confirmed. 'With you? I doubt it.'

'Never mind me. Just tell me about Eva.' He hunched his shoulders as he pressed the phone closer to his ear.

'How long are you going to do this to yourself, Roman?'

'Do what?'

'Stay away. Eva's a changed person since she came out to see you.'

'Changed how? Good? Bad?'

There was silence and then an impatient huff. 'Why don't you come back here and find out for yourself?'

'Too much to do and never enough time to do it.'

'That sounds like an excuse to me.'

'Everything sounds like an excuse to you. That's why we hired you to run the company.'

'Yeah, well, when it affects my family I'm even less amused. Come for the party, at least, Roman. Come and see what Eva has achieved here. Or is that too much to ask?'

He ground his jaw. No one gave him instructions. No one but the Skavanga Diamonds, he amended silently. 'I can't promise anything.'

'Yeah, that pretty much tallies with what Eva told me about you.'

'She confided in you?'

'She doesn't need to, Roman. She's my sister. I can read her like a book. So are you coming to the party or not?'

He stared into space for just long enough for Britt to exclaim something extremely unladylike.

'Okay, Britt, that's enough. I'll see you—'

'Not if I see you first,' she snapped.

He stared at the dead receiver in his hand. What

was it about these women? Were they born awkward, or did the frigid Arctic temperatures freeze the female gene out of them?

It didn't help that there was daily contact between him and Eva, and it was almost time for her mail. She was meticulous with her reports on progress at the mine. He studied them for the slightest hint that she was missing him, but had found no sign of that so far. Eva Skavanga, the most emotional woman he had ever known, had been transformed into a paragon of restraint and proper conduct. In fairness, she was doing a great job in Skavanga. And Britt was right. He was doing less well. According to his people on the ground, Eva had galvanised everyone into action, and the mining museum was now a reality under discussion with architects and geologists, rather than a pipe dream, and he had missed out on being part of the action.

So why was he sitting here in his office in Abu Dhabi, while Eva was half a world away in Skavanga?

Because it was business as usual and he hadn't lost his golden touch. He'd made a third fortune.

And his life was so full.

Staring at spreadsheets and bank balances really made up for the loss of Eva Skavanga in his life. Like hell it did! He missed her fire and temperament. He missed the chaos she brought to his life. And who listened to Eva's concerns? Had she made up with Britt? She must have done by now, he guessed. Was Leila home from university, or was Eva all on her own? He had people in Skavanga he could ask, but he couldn't bring himself to do that. He felt guilty enough already. He'd asked everything of Eva and had given her nothing but a job.

He brightened the moment he heard mail drop. It was that time of day. It had to be a mail from Eva with her latest report.

He scrolled down. Apparently, the money he'd pumped in had allowed them to create a garden around the mine. Good. She'd like that. Stretching his powerful limbs, he scanned the mail again, as if reading Eva's words could somehow bring her closer.

And this was the same woman he could cheerfully have given away with two camels and a coop of chickens as part of the deal when he'd first met her at Britt's wedding—a day that felt like another lifetime now. His life was dull without Eva. He'd seen what it could be like with her, and no other woman could hope to come close. He missed her. Just this contact between them over the internet raised his pulse and made him smile. He couldn't envisage life without her. He loved her. It was as simple, and as complicated, as that.

He craned forward as the computer pinged again.

From: Eva Skavanga
To: Roman Quisvada
Subject: Future challenges
Are we in danger of seeing you in Skavanga any time soon, or are the conditions here too challenging for you?

From: Roman Quisvada
To: Eva Skavanga
Subject: Mistaken assumptions
Hasty conclusions have never been your strong suit, Eva. Just remain focused on the job, or you're no use to me.

From: Eva Skavanga
To: Roman Quisvada
Subject: Are you firing me?

From: Roman Quisvada
To: Eva Skavanga
Subject: Firing you?
Hell, no! That would cost me money. Surely you know me better than that by now?

No, but she'd like to, Eva mused wryly, pushing her chair back as she got up from her desk and stretched. Email was a mixed blessing. The instant communication with someone half a world away was useful, but it was a soulless way to chat. She didn't want to keep staring at a screen that made the distance between them seem even more unbridgeable.

How was it possible to miss one man so much? How was it possible to mess up so badly? Her sisters were right. Her ridiculous pride was the only thing preventing her from speaking to Roman on a personal level—that and her even more ridiculous insecurities.

A gorgeous man with everything going for him, Leila had protested. Someone prepared to save our family business? And he gave you a job. And then Britt had started in, reminding Eva that thanks to Roman's restoration plans the mining museum was now a solid work-in-progress.

'You're a fool if you let him go,' Leila had flashed with unusual vigour. 'If your only ambition in life is to become a bitter old shrew, then you're well on your way.'

As if she needed to be told that. Perching on the sofa by the window, she buried her head in her hands.

Feeling sorry for herself lasted barely ten seconds before she remembered Britt telling her that life was precious and no one should waste a second of it.

It was time to call pest control and put that shrew firmly in its box.

She called Britt. 'That party tomorrow night to celebrate the revival of the mine?'

'So you're coming?' Britt sounded pleased.

'Of course, I'm coming.'

'So...? Look, if you're ringing me to ask if Roman will be there, I'm afraid I don't know.'

'You don't know, or you won't tell me?'

Her sister laughed. 'I don't know—honestly. I have no idea what Roman's timetable looks like. He doesn't share it with me.'

Or me, Eva thought.

'Just don't come dressed as one of the boys,' Britt suggested. 'The press will be there and they'll want to see the Skavanga Diamonds dressed to thrill now we're all involved in the running of the mine. And we could do with a decent family photograph—so no boiler suits, Eva. There are plenty of nice dress shops in Skavanga. I'll come along and help you pick something out, if you like?'

'Spare me,' Eva begged, imagining some interminable session with snooty assistants viewing her disparagingly, and a sister who had better things to do. It was just a shame she had no idea what constituted 'a nice dress'.

'Where is she?' he asked Leila, slipping the phone between his chin and his shoulder so he could open the door, speak on his cell and heft his case through the fire door without having it slam in his face. He had one thought in his mind, one thought only, and that was Eva.

'Why should I tell you?' Leila asked him with more honest curiosity in her voice than outright refusal.

'I think you know,' he said, glancing round the room to get his bearings.

'I know you hurt her, Count Quisvada. I know your absence bewilders her. And I also know that you're the only man, apart from our brother Tyr, who isn't frightened of my sister. But I'm going to ask you one last time, why do you need to know where Eva is?'

'Try this,' he said, dumping the case. 'Eva works for me and I need to catch up with her. Does that do it for you?'

'How about you miss her?' Leila countered. 'That might work for me. How about, you can't function without her, because my sister has taken up permanent residence in your head? That would also work for me.'

'And you're the quiet sister?'

Leila chose to ignore that. 'I know you have resources, Count Quisvada. Why don't you find her yourself?'

Because using them would take too much time. He wanted to see Eva now. Right this minute, Roman reflected impatiently as he lifted a slat on the blind at the window to stare out. 'I've tried all the usual numbers. She's not answering.'

'And suddenly it's an emergency?' Leila demanded sceptically.

'Yes, it is.' He missed Eva more than he could say and he wanted this conversation over with. Missed her was in fact a preposterous understatement. He couldn't think straight without her. He wanted Eva back in his arms where she belonged. He had driven her away and now he had every intention of making things right. He tried another tack. 'Come on, Leila,' he coaxed in what he hoped was a winning voice. 'I thought you were supposed to be the easy-going sister?'

'The pliable one, do you mean?' she said, surprising him with her heated response. 'Appearances can be deceptive, Count Quisvada.'

Tell my friend Raffa that, he thought, remembering the third man in the consortium's reaction when Raffa Leon had first caught sight of Leila's photograph. Raffa had thought the youngest Skavanga Diamond innocent and appealing. Roman had always thought her shrewder and more obstinate than she looked. Guess who'd been right?

'Call me Roman,' he said politely. 'And tell me where she is today. Please,' he added, holding on to his patience by the slimmest of threads. 'If you care anything about your sister, do it. And do it now. I need to find her, Leila.'

He closed his eyes and let out a long, relieved breath as Eva's sister finally dished up the information he craved.

'Are you still there?' Leila demanded.

'Thank you,' he whispered on autopilot, his mind full of Eva.

'Do you love her?'

That woke him up. 'Forgive me, Leila, but you're not going to be the first to hear how I feel about your sister. And now, if you will excuse me—'

He ended the call on some platitude or other. Urgency had entered his thinking when the plane landed, and it was at crisis point now. It wasn't enough to admit the word *love* and keep it to himself, he had to tell Eva face to face how he felt about her. And he had to do that right now.

CHAPTER SIXTEEN

SHE HAD TO accept that sometimes she made terrible choices, and that potentially this was one of those times. The assistants had just assured her that the tight blue dress with the bright pink collar looked amazing with Eva's flame-red hair and ivory complexion.

'As in, amazing I can look this bad?' she said, reaching for the back zip.

'As in let me do that for you…'

'Roman!'

'Eva,' he murmured, holding her stare.

Her world had just tilted on its axis. How could Roman Quisvada be standing right in front of her in a dress shop on the main street of Arctic Skavanga? No one knew she was shopping today…*except for her sisters.*

'What are you doing here?' she demanded as if he didn't have every right to be there.

'Window shopping.'

His voice was low and his stare was direct, while she wasn't even sure his name had made it to her lips, or that she'd even said hello properly.

And he was her boss, Eva reminded herself as she filled her eyes with him. The shock of seeing him had rendered her speechless. Tall, dark and preposterously handsome, Roman was standing in the doorway, muffled up in a dark ski jacket, jeans, boots and scarf, staring into her dazzled eyes. He was like the one fixed point in an increasingly uncertain reality. Even the assistants had backed away, and were cowering together as if they had never encountered such a powerful force. She didn't blame them. Roman wasn't someone you instinctively stepped in front of. Rather, you stood to one side in the hope that he didn't notice you. Unless you were Eva Skavanga, of course.

'That dress is hideous, Eva. I can't imagine why you're wearing it. We're leaving,' he added. 'I've seen something better down the street.'

'You have?' she said, shooting sympathetic glances at the hovering assistants.

'I'm booked in across the road at the hotel,' he explained, 'and I saw you come in here. You're looking for something to wear at the party tomorrow—'

'And that's why you're here?'

'That's one of the reasons,' he said. 'Turn around so I can get you out of that thing.'

Eva was sure she heard a collective sigh rise from the cringing assistants as Roman slid the zipper down her back.

'Now go put your clothes on,' he said with all the confidence of a master of seduction. 'I'm going to take you to buy a dress.'

'I don't need you to buy me anything,' she protested, having recovered slightly from the shock. 'And,' she began as he ushered her through the door and out of the shop.

'And I've been away too long,' he suggested.

As his mouth crashed down on hers she could only agree. Backing her up against the plate-glass window, Roman pinned her in position with his hands on either side of her face. She was vaguely aware of the assistants with their faces practically glued to the glass behind them.

'Are you determined to make a spectacle out of me?' she demanded when he finally released her.

Roman's answer was to smile, and when he yanked her close this time she didn't waste time trying to push him away, she just laced her fingers through his hair and responded.

'Are we going to make it to the party?' she murmured, speaking her thoughts out loud.

'I very much doubt it as we've only got a little over twenty-four hours.'

'But the dress—'

'I'll have it delivered,' he said, steering her safely across the road.

'How do we know it will fit?'

'I've made an educated guess,' he said, leading her step by wicked step towards the brilliantly lit hotel entrance. 'I've taken a suite—'

'No. Seriously?' she said, making them both smile as her gaze fixed on Roman's sexy mouth.

'With a very big bed,' he murmured as they waited for the elevator.

'I'd expect nothing less.'

'As well as all sorts of other possibilities, should you choose to be adventurous,' he added as the steel doors slid open.

'I'm sure I shall be.' Her heart was beating so fast

she wondered if it would be possible to draw her next breath as Roman swiped his room card in the control panel. 'The penthouse floor?' she confirmed.

'Unless you'd like to do some sightseeing along the way?'

He had already pressed the button to stop the lift, and before the machinery even had a chance to obey his hand was on her and Roman was undoing his zipper.

'Let me take them off,' she insisted, struggling frantically with the waistband of her briefs.

'I've got a better idea.'

She shrieked with excitement as they hit the floor.

'Don't worry, we'll add underwear to the dress order,' Roman soothed, pressing her back against the cool steel wall.

'Or maybe I'll just stop wearing underwear. I mean, what's the point?'

'No point,' he agreed, lifting her.

She barely had time to wrap her legs around his waist before he cupped her buttocks and entered her, sinking deep to the hilt. She lost control at once, and the enclosed space resounded with her screams of release.

'Greedy,' Roman murmured, moving steadily to get the best out of her.

'Are you kidding?' she said, having calmed enough to speak. 'I haven't even got started yet.'

Roman laughed, a deep, contented rumble she could feel through his polar jacket.

'Again,' she insisted in a fierce whisper as he made the mistake of reaching for the lift button.

He slammed into her and they used all their considerable combined strength to reach the conclusion they both needed so desperately, as quickly as they could.

Her screams this time could probably be heard in Rome. She didn't care. She was only glad Roman had the presence of mind to take charge, and move the lift on.

'Before we break the cables,' he explained.

He let her down gently, steadying her on her feet as the elevator started to move again. Retrieving her ruined briefs, she stuffed them in her pocket as the steel doors slid wide. A small, private lobby, elegantly decorated in understated Skandi-style, faced them as they approached a sleek beech wood door leading into the penthouse suite.

'This door looks solid,' Roman murmured as he let them in.

'You're just taking advantage of the fact that I'm not wearing any underwear,' Eva commented wryly as Roman tugged off his jacket and tossed it on a chair.

'You bet I am.'

Yes, the door was solid. They proved that conclusively. And Roman was efficient. With a few, deep, well-judged thrusts, he pushed her over the edge again.

'This isn't fair. What about you?' she gasped, clutching him as she dragged in some necessary breaths.

'The floor?' he suggested.

'That rug looks soft,' she agreed. 'Like this?'

'Perfect,' Roman murmured, dropping to his knees behind her.

And, oh, it was perfect. She lifted her bottom as high as she could, while he controlled her with his hands, taking firm hold of the soft, plump flesh. She felt so gloriously exposed, and he was so gloriously skilful. He sank deep, and knew just how to touch her.

'Open your legs a little more for me, Eva.'

She did so and let out a shaking cry as Roman found

her with one finger and began to circle the most demanding part of her.

'So soon?' he demanded, knowing full well she couldn't hold on.

She didn't have time to answer him, and could only wail her appreciation in time to the violent bolts of sensation, while she rested with her face pressed into the soft fur rug.

'And now the bed?' she suggested when she could find her voice.

'It's too far away. And now the sofa,' Roman argued, tugging his shirt over his head.

Arranging her with her hips balanced on the very edge of the seat, he knelt in front of her, and, lifting her legs onto his shoulders, where the wide spread of his body kept them well apart, he braced his arms against the back of the cushions.

'It's my pleasure to serve you,' he said, teasing her with just the tip.

'Serve away,' she encouraged, groaning with pleasure as he thrust inside her and began to move. 'Again,' she screamed, losing herself in the moment.

They almost made it to the bed, but not quite, as a console table with a handy mirror on the wall behind it got in their way. It proved to have a very firm surface indeed and provided them with a welcome diversion on their way to more pleasure on the bed.

They made it to the party. Just. Eva in an ivory silk off-the-shoulder dress that made her feel like a princess for a night, and Roman in a dark dress suit that still managed to make him look like a marauding pirate with his thick ink-black hair, deep tan and disreputable stubble.

There had barely been time for bathing, dressing, hopping round on spindly heels while she tried to arrange the ankle strap on each foot, before Roman yelled that it was time to leave. And as for him—just enough time to rake his still-damp hair as they waited for the elevator to arrive, and there had not been time for him to shave. Not that she was complaining. She loved him just the way he was, and looked on proudly as, after hugging Eva as if they had been parted for years, Britt introduced Roman as a leading member of the consortium responsible for reviving the fortunes of both the mine and the town that bore their name.

'And none of it would have been possible without the Skavanga Diamonds,' Roman finished up by saying. 'And I'm not talking about lumps of carbon we claw from the earth, but these girls: Britt, Leila, and Eva Skavanga, without whose dogged determination I might never have parted with so much money.' And as everyone laughed, he added in a murmur to Eva, 'Or my heart.'

'And as proof positive that the consortium couldn't possibly work as well as it does without the Skavanga sisters, this is the right time for me to tell you that from now on Britt Skavanga will be the President of Skavanga Mining, while Eva Skavanga will officially be our roving consultant when it comes to ecological concerns and cultural development,' he ended to a chorus of enthusiastic cheers.

As everyone peeled away and the band started to play, Roman drew her aside.

'Did you consult me?' she said.

'Do you want the job or not?'

'Are you kidding? You know I do. It's all I've ever dreamed of.'

'That's what I thought.'

'And sometimes it's nice to get a surprise,' she admitted.

'Well, I'll have to see what else I can do to surprise you.'

'Please,' she said.

'The first thing is this,' he said, delving in his pocket.

'Your gold chain?' She was speechless.

'I think it will look better on you than it looks on me.'

'Oh, Roman...' Emotion overcame her and she was lost for words for a moment as he fastened the precious chain around her neck.

'I've got something else for you.'

'And what's that?' She frowned as Roman drew her deeper into the shadows at the side of the impromptu stage.

'Your bonus,' he said.

'I thought I already had that,' she teased as they smiled into each other's eyes.

'It is usual to reward particularly successful staff.'

'I'm very glad I pleased you, sir,' she said, bobbing him a mock curtsy.

'Oh, you did. You do. So now I want you to accept this.'

'What is it?' she said, unfolding the sheet of paper.

'A flight plan to Rome.'

'Are you serious?'

'Never more so. I love you, Eva Skavanga. I love you more than life itself. And I did warn you what would happen if you tossed that coin into the fountain. We have to go back to Rome. What? You don't want to?' He was surprised by the look on Eva's face.

'Can't you get someone else to fly the plane?'

'Yes.' He frowned. 'Why? Don't you trust me to get us there safely?'

'Of course I do, but I've got plans for you, and, adventurous though we are, I don't think we should risk the cockpit. You never know what I might sit on.'

'I've got a pretty good idea.' And taking hold of her hand, he held her gaze with his wicked eyes as he raised her fingers to his lips.

EPILOGUE

BEING CONTRARY, EVA got everything the wrong way around, and so they took a honeymoon in Rome before they got married on the island. They travelled in Roman's private jet and, as planned, they sampled every surface that would support them along the way, and a few that threatened not to do so, especially when turbulence intervened, tipping them both up hard against the bulkhead.

'Remind me never to listen to your suggestions again,' Roman said as he picked her up and set her down on his knee. 'These are perfectly decent seats. Why don't we use them?'

'All of them?' Eva raised an optimistic brow as she glanced around the cabin.

Roman shot a look at his watch. 'There should be time.'

'Don't you dare short-change me,' she warned.

'And don't push me, lady, or I might have to work on instilling more discipline into you.'

'Than you already have? Oh, please,' she purred. 'Discipline's exactly what's been missing from my life all these years, but thankfully that's changed now. Shall I position myself over your knee?'

'Later, I think. There's something I must do first.'

'Won't it wait?'

'Straddle me and find out.'

'Must I?'

'I think you must.'

She heaved a sigh. 'How do the cabin attendants know when to make themselves scarce, by the way?'

'There's a call button?' Roman informed her patiently.

'We haven't given them much to do.'

'If you're hungry—'

'Oh, I am,' she assured him. 'But I very much doubt they carry what I need in the galley.'

'Almost certainly not,' he agreed. 'Are you sitting comfortably?'

Her answer was to throw back her head and sigh with delight.

'Then I'll begin…'

They travelled by private launch to the island, where they were to get married at sunset on the beach, surrounded by friends and family. Leila was the first person to greet them on the jetty. Eva's younger sister seemed flushed and unusually animated as they hugged, and it didn't take Eva long to work out why. The answer came at supper that evening, when the sisters and the three men in the consortium met for a celebratory meal on the night before the wedding.

Sheikh Sharif was of course married to Eva's sister Britt, and Roman was definitely spoken for, but Raffa Leon, the frighteningly brutal-looking Duke of Cantalabria, was reportedly unattached, and it made Eva's heart judder with apprehension to see her gentle little sister choose a seat opposite the grim-faced duke.

Why? Eva wondered as she watched Leila field the duke's acerbic commentary with thoughtful observations of her own. Why must opposites attract?

The tension between Leila and the duke was like a blazing flame that would consume her sister. Eva wanted someone softer and more compliant for quiet little Leila, not some rampaging barbarian from a rugged mountain range in some far distant corner of Europe. The duke might be an aristocrat, but in name only, in Eva's opinion. His eyes were hard and unforgiving, and his manner was borderline aggressive. His manners were good enough, but she soon worked out that everyone, apart from Roman and Sheikh Sharif, was more than a little wary of the Spanish grandee. And with good cause, she thought as Raffa pushed away from the table with some cursory excuse.

And good riddance to you, she thought, irritated to see Leila's gaze follow the Spanish duke to the door. The other two men soon found a reason to join him and leave the Skavanga sisters to discuss the wedding.

'Let me see your ring,' Leila begged.

Telling herself to calm down, and that her sister was a big girl now, who could take care of herself, Eva refocused on the most important event of her life. 'I don't need a ring to get married. That's such an old-fashioned concept.'

'Uh-oh, what's wrong?' Britt stared at Eva. 'I can't believe you just said that. You do know what industry we're in? We *mine* diamonds?' Britt exchanged a concerned glance with Leila. 'So what do you mean, you don't need a ring, Eva?' Britt demanded, flashing her own multi-carat whopper. 'What's going to happen when the official asks for the rings to marry you?'

'Well, I've got Roman's ring here,' Eva protested, revealing the plain platinum band she and Roman had chosen together.

'Yes. Very nice,' Britt agreed, 'but what about your wedding band?'

'Or are you going all Boho, and using a lock of his hair to tie around your finger?' Leila suggested, flashing anxious glances between her sisters.

'Don't be so ridiculous,' Eva flared. 'I only need Roman.'

Eva felt her throat dry on the lie, realising the subject of her wedding band hadn't even figured in her discussions with Roman. It seemed they had both forgotten. In her heart of hearts she had been hoping for a surprise, but it was too late for that now.

The morning of the wedding dawned bright and sunny, and, though it seemed a long time until the sunset ceremony on the beach, the day was packed with so much to do that it seemed five minutes since Eva had last caught sight of Roman as he left after supper the night before.

'I wish you had a ring,' Leila fretted, always the one to think of other people before herself. 'Are you sure you're not upset about it?'

'Not a bit,' Eva said briskly.

'Anyway, it's too late to worry about it now,' Britt observed as she tweaked the hem of Eva's ankle-length ivory silk dress. 'You look beautiful, by the way. And you're right. You don't need a ring. All you need is the man you love.'

'Says you, with a hand you can hardly lift up, it's so weighted down by diamonds,' Leila observed wryly.

'And any man who can tame you, Eva, should be thinking in terms of fur-lined handcuffs and other delicious devices to bring you back into line when you get in one of your moods, not just a ring,' Britt continued unabashed.

They all laughed wildly—a little too wildly, quite possibly in Eva's case. Wedding fever, she convinced herself as she led the procession of Skavanga sisters towards the flower festooned canopy set out on the beach. She had no intention of sharing her intimate bedroom secrets with anyone, not even her sisters.

Roman was waiting for her, looking more gorgeous than ever, if such a thing were possible.

'And the rings?' the woman who was going to marry them prompted as Eva handed her bouquet of orchids to Leila.

Leila bit her lip and heaved a worried sigh as she carefully positioned the platinum band Roman would wear on the crimson velvet cushion.

The woman waited, and then prompted, 'May I have both the rings, please?'

'Oh, forgive me…'

All three sisters turned to look at Roman, who was rummaging in his pocket. 'Will these do?'

Eva gasped as Roman tipped two fabulous rings onto the cushion.

'I'm sorry there's been a delay,' he explained discreetly, 'but you know I'm a stickler for design and cut. The stones are the finest quality and have the distinction of being amongst the first batch to be taken from the Skavanga mine. You do like them?' he prompted when Eva remained speechless.

She wondered if her voice would work. The rings were fabulous. There was a slim platinum wedding band encrusted with diamonds, and a truly incredible solitaire cut in the shape of a heart. It was not what a tomboy would automatically choose, but it was a far better choice than she could ever make. 'It's… They're… Sorry…I'm just lost for words.'

'The only thing that matters is that they fit,' Roman exclaimed with relief as he placed the wedding band on her finger.

'It's so beautiful,' Eva breathed, holding her hand up so that the diamonds flashed fire.

'And the finishing touch,' Roman reminded her as he slipped the diamond heart on her wedding finger. 'Not too much—'

'And definitely not too little,' Britt piped up as they all stared in awestruck wonder at the fabulous gems.

'I love you, Eva Skavanga,' Roman declared, bringing her hand to his lips. 'And no jewel could ever be good enough for you.'

'You may kiss the bride,' the official said.

And as everyone stood back and applauded, Eva murmured, 'I love you too.' But as their kiss grew more heated she found a moment to whisper discreetly, 'Can't we just slip away to bed?'

'When I tell you…you can,' Roman promised wickedly in the same muted tone.

'I might right here,' she warned him.

'What's your hurry, Eva?' Roman murmured. 'Haven't I taught you the benefits of delay? It's not like we're short of time. We've got for ever. Remember?'

'For ever isn't nearly long enough,' she complained, but Roman wasn't in the mood to let the old Eva Skavanga raise her fiery head, and so he drew Eva into his arms and silenced her the best way he knew, which was very thoroughly with a kiss.

* * * * *